Finding My Baby

The Reunited Series

By

Rose Bak

FINDING MY BABY
© 2022 by Rose Bak

Table of Contents

About This Book

Emily Langdon thought she'd put the past behind her...until a letter from the adoption agency changes everything.

Single and child-free, Emily has spent most of her life focused on her career, resigned to never having a family. But now the baby Emily put up for adoption twenty-one years ago wants to meet her, which means telling her daughter the painful truth about what happened in college.

Brian McKenna is like another father to his niece Jane, so when he learns that she's found her birth mother, he's determined to keep her from getting hurt again. As he gets to know Emily, he realizes that his niece isn't the only one who's found someone to love.

If only they can both break through Emily's protective walls...

"Finding My Baby" is the second book in the Reunited Series. Each book in the series is a steamy standalone midlife romance featuring a mature couple, meddling best friends, impossible reunions, and a guaranteed happily ever after.

Note: "Finding My Baby" includes references to past events that some readers may find triggering.

This book includes a special excerpt from "Until You Came Along", book one of the Oliver Boys Band series, available now from all major online retailers.

Be sure to join Rose's mailing list and get a free book. Click here[1] to be the first to hear about all the latest releases and special sales.

---

1. https://storyoriginapp.com/giveaways/62ee758e-068f-11eb-904e-c373f6014fe1

Dedication

To all the survivors.

Prologue – Brian

Three months ago...

"Thanks for coming with me Brian."

Lainie wrapped her hand around Brian McKenna's arm as they waited for the bar line to move.

"I know it's stupid, but I hate to come to these things alone and look like a loser."

"It's not stupid and you're not a loser," he told his friend firmly. "You haven't seen most of these people in twenty-five years. They're basically strangers."

Brian had agreed to be Lainie's date for her twenty-fifth high school reunion. She had gone to school in the suburbs somewhere, but the reunion was a big fancy event at one of the big hotels in downtown Chicago.

He was glad to do his friend a favor. He only lived a short subway ride away from here, and there was fancy food and an open bar. Plus, a reunion would provide prime people watching opportunities. There was always drama at these things.

"You look beautiful, by the way. I'm sure all the guys who ignored you in high school are going to be regretting that decision now."

He gave her a warm smile and wished, not for the first time, that he felt a spark with Lainie. She was everything he wanted in a life partner: successful, independent, confident in her skin, loved sports. In fact, the two of them were part of a group of friends who shared season tickets for the Cubs, one of Chicago's two baseball teams.

Lainie also really wanted to be a mom, and that wasn't something Brian was interested in at this point in his life. He had put his personal life on hold for the last few years to raise his niece after her parents died, but now that she was done with college, had a good job, and had moved out on her own, he was ready to think about having a relationship. He wasn't totally opposed to having kids, but at forty-five it felt like it was a little late.

The two friends mingled for a while, eating hors d'oevres and catching up with some of Lainie's old classmates. They seemed like a nice group of people, but then again he was a bit of an extravert and felt comfortable talking to strangers.

The organizers announced that dinner was ready, and they all moved to the tables that ringed the conference room. Heaping platters of food were served family style while waiters hovered around topping off wine glasses.

The friends all reminisced about high school while Brian looked around. His eye caught on a beautiful blonde at the next table, and he felt an unexpected pull towards her, like she was someone he needed to know. He wondered if they'd met before, something about her seemed kind of familiar.

The woman turned and pointed her finger at some guy talking to the lady next to her, her expression stormy. He couldn't hear what they were saying, but the woman appeared to be telling him off or warning him about something. When Brian looked back later the guy was gone, along with the woman who'd been sitting next to the elegant blonde.

After dinner they lowered the lights and replaced the background music with some favorites from when they were kids. People started gravitating towards the dance floor in the middle of the room, and it didn't take long for someone to approach Lainie and ask her to dance. She'd pointed him out earlier as a boy she'd had a crush on in high school, so Brian wasn't surprised when Lainie accepted his invitation to hit the dance floor. She knew him well enough to know that Brian wouldn't mind if she left him alone for a while.

He stood on the side of the room, people watching, and noticed that the blonde from earlier was standing alone. Seal's "A Kiss from a Rose" started and Brian headed in her direction. As he got closer he could see that she was stunning.

Everything about her screamed cool elegance. Her blonde hair fell halfway between her chin and shoulders in a stylish bob. She was white, with pale skin, blue eyes, a sharp chin, and Cupid's bow lips, painted a dark pink.

She was a little tall for a woman, maybe five foot six, although her high heeled shoes brought her a little closer to his height. An expensive looking blue dress, almost a perfect match for her eyes, hugged her curves, but he could see from her bare arms and legs that she was fit and muscular. She was exquisite.

"May I have this dance?" he asked.

The woman shot him a surprised smile, then said, "Sure".

He wondered how often that coolness she projected kept men from approaching her. She was stunning, but something about her screamed "untouchable".

He took her hand and felt a shock of awareness rush through him as their palms met. Brian led her to the crowded dance floor, pulling her into his arms. They fit perfectly together. He placed his hands on her waist as she slid her hands up to his shoulders, and they started swaying together to the old song. He inhaled and smelled the sweet scent of citrus of her shampoo.

The music was too loud here to talk, so they just smiled at each other and enjoyed the music. She had a beautiful smile and this close, he could see the flawlessness of her skin, only marred by faint laugh lines around her eyes. Her blue eyes were shadowed though, like she'd seen a lot of pain in her life. He wondered what her story was and felt an odd sense of protectiveness towards her.

The song ended and he debated asking her for a second dance. A quick look around confirmed that Lainie was still dancing with her old crush so it wouldn't be a problem. He pulled her closer as the next song started, and she moved towards him with a sigh.

Suddenly another woman rushed up to them, interrupting. Brian recognized her as one of the women his dance partner had been sitting with at dinner.

"Emily, thank god, I need to get out of here!"

The woman – Emily apparently – stopped dancing and turned to her friend. "What's wrong Amber?"

"Andy Sosnowski is what's wrong. He's completely insane! Talking about love and marriage like it hasn't been twenty-five years since we've seen each other. Can we find Jenny and leave? Please?"

"Of course honey." Emily looked up at him with a sweet smile, her eyes filled with the same regret he felt. "I have to go. Thanks for the dance though. I hope you enjoy the rest of the reunion."

Emily

Dear Ms. Langdon,

We are reaching out to advise you that the child you entrusted to the Sisters of Harmony adoption program has contacted us in an effort to locate her birth parents. In accordance with the agreement you signed with us and Illinois state law, now that the child is an adult they are eligible to receive the details of their adoption, including names and known contact information of their biological parents.

Your biological daughter, now known as Jane Marie Scott, will likely be contacting you. While it is your decision whether to meet your child, in most cases both the birth parents and the adopted child find that meeting each other can be a positive experience. We know that this letter and any subsequent contact between you and your child may be difficult to process emotionally and we encourage you to talk to a qualified counselor or priest on how to best navigate the process. We can provide you a list of counselors in your area at your request.

Please do not hesitate to contact us if you have questions or need additional information.

Sincerely,

Sister Mary Magdalina

Director of Adoption Services

Emily slid down the wall as the letter fell from her hands. Her butt hit the stone tile in her foyer, and she struggled to breathe. When she'd opened her mailbox and saw the official looking letter, she had known right away it was something big. There was only a P.O. Box as the return address, no indication that the letter was from the Sisters of Harmony until she'd actually opened it, but somehow she'd known. She'd been expecting this ever since her daughter turned twenty-one a couple of months ago.

Funny how all these years of wondering if this would happen did nothing to prepare her for it. She ran shaky fingers through her shoulder-length blonde hair. Damn it. Her life was about to get upended – again – because of one bad decision she'd made in college.

She had thought of this day for years. Wondered how she would feel. She'd imagined that she would be happy or sad or... something besides what she felt right now. Numb. Of course numb was her "go to" for difficult situations, a defense mechanism she'd learned years ago.

She wondered when her daughter would contact her. Or even if she would contact her. Emily had heard that sometimes adopted kids got the information about their birth parents and did a little sleuthing to learn about them, but never made actual contact.

If Jane made contact, she would undoubtedly ask about her father. How on earth was she going to look this young woman in the eye and tell her the truth about what happened? If the shoe were on the other foot and she was looking for her birth parents, she would be devastated by the truth.

Emily wondered if she'd made a mistake all those years ago when she agreed that her child could have the records unsealed when she became of age. Of course she wasn't obligated to respond if her daughter contacted her. She could just ignore Jane if she reached out. But that would be a horrible thing to do to the girl.

What if Jane just showed up at her house one day without notice? That would we awkward. Emily felt nauseous. She pressed her hand against her abdomen, as if that would make the queasiness go away.

Reaching around, she found the purse that she had dropped when she'd opened the letter. Sliding out her phone, she stared at the screen blankly before unlocking it and texting the two women she'd been best friends with since freshman year of high school.

She and Jenny and Amber had maintained their unlikely friendship throughout the dramas of high school and college, and all the years since then. They were the only ones who knew the truth about what happened. The only ones who knew what it had cost her to make the most agonizing decision a woman should ever have to make. They were also the only ones who stood by her during that dark time.

She hesitated for a moment. No doubt Jenny would be with her boyfriend Dave and Amber would be with supposedly-platonic friend Andy, enjoying some "benefits". The two couples had reunited at their twenty-fifth high school reunion a few months ago. They were all in that "new relationship" phase where they wanted to spend every minute together.

She felt bad about bothering them, but Emily knew that they would come if she needed them, no questions asked. After receiving the letter, she needed her friends. She unlocked her phone and opened their group chat.

Emily: *Are you girls busy?*
Amber: *Just getting off work, whatcha need?*
Jenny: *I'm at Dave's. Are you OK?*
Emily: *I need you girls. 911*
Jenny: *I'll be there in 15 minutes.*
Emily: *It's big*
Jenny: *I'll bring alcohol, Dave's got a stash of the good stuff*
Amber: *I'll grab us some food and be there in 30.*

She put down the phone and smiled. Her friends were the best thing that had ever happened to her. They would help her get through this, the same way they'd all been helping each other navigate life's ups and downs for almost thirty years.

Emily forced herself to get up off the floor. No sense sitting there. She moved through her townhouse, looking around with fresh eyes and imagining what her daughter would see if she came here.

She owned a nice two-bedroom townhouse in Evanston, just north of the city. Although she teleworked a couple of days a week, she also lived close enough that she could easily take public transportation her office in downtown Chicago.

Emily had purchased the place with a down payment from her first big bonus. She'd been recruited right after college by a large international business consulting company, and she had worked there ever since. She liked the work, and the pay and benefits were generous. By now she was high enough in the company that she could easily afford a nicer place, maybe something on the Gold Coast, but she liked her little place in her quiet neighborhood.

Her home was warm and inviting, decorated with earth tones and comfortable furniture. The cozy space suited her. One of the best features was a "sunroom" off the main bedroom which she had repurposed into a home office. The space was just large enough to hold a desk and filing cabinet, and it allowed her to look out through the large windows while she worked. If she crooked her head she could even see the glimmer of the lake over the neighboring rooftops.

She wondered what her daughter's life had been like. Had she had a good childhood? Had she gone to college? Was she angry that Emily had given her up for adoption? God, she had no idea how to navigate this situation. Maybe she should talk to a counselor like program manager suggested.

Kicking off the heels she wore for work, Emily traded her pencil skirt and blouse for yoga pants, an old t-shirt, and a pair of socks that were decorated with cartoon chickens – a gift from her friend Amber. Amber liked to off-set Emily and Jenny's professional wardrobes with funny socks and shirts, telling them it kept them from getting "too stuffy".

The doorbell rang, signaling that arrival of her friends. She would feel better after she talked to them. She always did.

Brian

"Hey Uncle Brian!"

Brian looked up with a smile as his niece Jane came racing across the restaurant towards him. He stood up and enveloped her in a big hug, kissing the top of her blonde head. He'd always been close to the girl, but since her parents died a few years ago, their relationship had become even closer.

Jane had only been fourteen when they'd died, a freshman in high school, and Brian had become her guardian. She'd lived with him for her the rest of high school and throughout college while she'd been attending Northwestern, but after she'd graduated this summer she'd moved into an apartment in the city with two of her girlfriends.

She'd only been gone for three months, but he already missed having her around his house every day. It was funny how he the house had never felt that empty all those years he'd lived alone before she came to live with him.

"How's it going pumpkin?" he asked, using the nickname he'd given her when her parents had brought her home from the adoption agency all those years ago. She had been so tiny back then, but now she was a grown woman.

She looked even more grown up today, dressed in the slim fit pants, blouse, and professional heels she wore to work at the investment firm, her blonde hair smoothed back into a sedate bun. It was too bad his sister and her husband hadn't lived long enough to see their baby all grown up.

They both worked downtown and had decided to meet at one of the myriad of restaurants that served the busy city. It was surreal meeting his grown-up niece after work, both of them dressed professionally and navigating the after-work dinner crowd.

"I have big news," she told him as she fiddled with her silverware. "But let's order first."

They chatted comfortably until the waiter took their order. Conversation had always been easy between them. He eyed his niece drinking a glass of wine and smiled to himself. She really was grown up now. After all, she'd turned twenty-one in June, right after she graduated college.

After the waiter departed he looked at her expectantly. "Tell me your news."

Jane took another small sip of her wine and leaned forward excitedly. "I heard back from the adoption agency. I found my mom."

Brian nodded and tried not to show any of the emotions he was feeling. Jane had never mentioned finding her birth parents until after her adoptive parents had been killed. When she'd found out that she had to wait until she was twenty-one to get the records unsealed, she had been disappointed.

He wasn't sure if his sister and his husband had ever discussed this with Jane, but he suspected that part of her eagerness to find her birth parents was related to losing her adoptive parents at such a young age. He only hoped she wouldn't regret starting the process. He'd heard horror stories about adoption reunifications that went wrong.

Jane removed a folder from her briefcase and opened up to the papers inside. "My birth mother's name is Emily Langdon. She's forty-three years old and she lives here, or in Evanston anyway. She's some kind of business consultant, pretty high up in her company. She runs 5ks and likes the opera. Oh, and she's a Cubs fan."

"They told you all that?" he asked. He didn't realize the adoption agency would keep tabs on the biological parents like that.

Jane shook her head and laughed. "No. They just gave me a packet with a copy of my original birth certificate, the adoption decree, and my birth mother's name and last known address. But thanks to the miracle of the internet, I was able to do some more research about her. As far as I can tell, she's not married and doesn't have any other kids. There's no pictures or references to them on her social media anyway."

Jane grabbed her phone and tapped on an icon. "This is her."

She showed him a picture of a woman with the same blonde hair and blue eyes that his niece had. It was a professional head shot on the website of the consulting company she apparently worked for. His breath caught. She was beautiful. She looked familiar, probably because there was such a strong resemblance between her and Jane. Clearly his niece took after her mother.

"What about your birth father?" he asked curiously. "Did they give you any information about him?"

"My original birth certificate says the father is unknown." Jane frowned. "I wonder why."

"It could be anything," he answered. "She really might not have known. It could have been a bad relationship. Or maybe your father was married or something and she was protecting him. You'll have to ask her about it."

Jane chewed her lip, a habit she had when she was nervous. "What if I contact her and she tells me she doesn't want to see me?" she asked. "I mean, she agreed to be contacted, but that was twenty-one years ago. In that Facebook adoption group I'm in, a few people have found their birth parents and had bad experiences. Some parents have been total losers, like drug addicts or criminals, and others have been super hostile about being contacted."

"You definitely need to prepare for that," Brian said carefully. "Then again, maybe she's been hoping to hear from you all these years. You'll never know until you talk to her. Just remember that whatever happens you'll be OK."

"I hope you don't think that this feels like an insult to my parents," Jane said. "They meant a lot to me, and you know that they were always open about the fact that I was adopted. I was always grateful that they adopted me, but when I was younger we all agreed that someday when I was old enough I would try to find out where I came from."

"I get it Janey, I really do," he reassured her. "I didn't realize you had all talked about it, but I would probably feel the same if I were you."

They paused as the waiter delivered their food, eating quietly for a few minutes. Finally he broke the silence.

"I know you said you wanted to know where you come from, but is that all this is about? Or are you hoping to find more family?"

Jane looked thoughtful. "It would be nice to find more family, that's for sure. You know I love you Uncle Brian, but it's just been the two of us for a long time. I'm super curious to see if I have any brothers and sisters. I always wanted a sister. Also it's probably good to get a family history, find out if there's any genetic diseases or anything that I should be worried about when I start my own family."

Brian tried not to grimace at the thought of some guy impregnating his niece. He knew she was an adult now, but that didn't mean he stopped feeling protective. "Hopefully that's a long way off," he said mildly.

Jane rolled her eyes. "I'm not even dating anyone right now, don't worry."

He felt relieved.

"I'm also just really curious about what the circumstances were. My parents always told me that my birth mother giving me up for adoption was a gift, a gift to people like them who couldn't have kids of their own, and a gift to a baby who had a chance for a better life. But now that I know that my birth mother is a professional with a good job, it makes me even more curious about why she didn't keep me."

"Are you upset with her for giving you up?"

"Oh no, not at all. I'm so grateful for the time I had with my parents. I just...I want to know my origin story. I want to know about my past."

"Well pumpkin, I hope you get the answers you're looking for."

"What should I do, Uncle Brian?" Jane asked. "Should I send her a letter or an email or how should I approach her? It seems rude to just show up on her doorstep with no warning."

"I guess I would suggest that send her a letter with your contact information and ask her to meet you. That way if she doesn't respond or she tells you no, at least you'll know where she stands."

Jane nodded. His normally confident niece seemed suddenly vulnerable, and he resolved to learn more about this Emily Langdon. Jane had been through enough already. There was no way he was going to allow someone else to hurt the girl who'd become like a daughter to him.

Emily

"Emily, your four o'clock appointment is here."

Emily stood and smoothed her skirt down. "Thanks Alicia. Please show him in."

Her assistant returned a few minutes later, a tall blonde man behind her. Smiling, Emily stepped forward around her desk and reached out her hand.

"Mr. McKenna, I'm Emily Langdon. It's nice to meet you."

"Brian McKenna. Nice to meet you Ms. Langdon."

"Please call me Emily."

He smiled and she caught her breath. "In that case, please call me Brian."

As the man's large hand engulfed her smaller one, Emily caught her breath. A fissure of awareness traveled up her arm, almost like a little electrical current. She looked up and met his warm brown eyes.

He was a handsome man white man, probably in his early to mid-forties, based on those little crinkles around his eyes. He was clean shaven, which she appreciated. It seemed like every guy was scruffy nowadays. His features were sharp but not harsh, and when her gaze landed on his lips they curled up just a bit on one side in a crooked grin. He was at least six inches taller than her own five foot six, with wide shoulders and a trim waist that was evident beneath the navy blue suit that hugged his frame.

Brian looked around her office, shrewd eyes taking in the expensive but understated furnishings and the artwork on the wall before returning to meet her gaze. His gaze felt...disconcerting, but she couldn't say why. He looked vaguely familiar, but she wasn't sure why. Maybe she'd seen him around town.

"Please, have a seat," she said, gesturing to the seating area. "Can we get you anything to drink?"

"No thank you," he responded politely. He dropped into a seat at one end of the small oval conference table she kept in her office for smaller client meetings. Emily sat across from him, picking up a pen to jot down some notes on the pad she kept there.

"Thank you for coming today Brian. I understand you're looking for a consultant for your auditing firm? I didn't catch what firm you're with."

When he didn't immediately answer, Emily looked up from her notebook to find him watching her with an intense look on his face. She suppressed a shiver, and shifted in her seat, pressing her thighs together tightly. She suddenly wished that she had met this guy in a non-work setting. It had been a long time since she'd been so attracted to someone.

He took a deep breath. "I have a confession to make Emily. I made this appointment under false pretenses," he said. "I don't actually need a consultant."

She frowned and stiffened in her seat. "Excuse me?"

"I'm here for a personal matter actually. I apologize for the ruse, but I wasn't sure you would meet with me otherwise."

She put her pen down and met his eyes, knowing that her irritation was clear on her face.

"What's this about then? Is Brian McKenna even your real name, or was that a fabrication too?"

She felt peeved. She hated subterfuge. Who was this guy? A process server? A private investigator? She couldn't imagine why this man would want to meet with her, unless...

"It's about your daughter, Jane. The one you gave up for adoption twenty-one years ago."

Her breath left her body in a whoosh, and she began nibbling on her lip. Her daughter had hired a private investigator to spy on her? That didn't make sense. It had only been a few days since she had received the letter from the adoption agency, and she hadn't even heard from her daughter yet. Unless her daughter wanted to check her out first before making contact?

Emily had been on pins and needles ever since she received the letter. Every time she looked at her phone or her email, she wondered when she would hear from Jane—and dreading the conversation she knew they would need to have...

"Are you a P.I.?" she asked, her voice cold.

The man laughed ruefully. "Oh no, nothing like that. I'm sorry, I think I'm messing this all up. My name really is Brian McKenna. I'm Jane's uncle. My sister and her husband were Jane's adoptive parents."

"Oh." She wasn't sure how to respond to this.

"Jane doesn't know I'm here, but I saw her last night and she shared the news that her records had been unsealed, and she shared information that she got about you from the adoption agency. She's really excited to meet her birth parents, but she she's been through a lot the last few years. I guess, well, I know I shouldn't violate her privacy like this, but I really wanted to meet you before she reached out to you and make sure that, um..."

"That I'm not crazy?" Emily asked. "Or some terrible person?"

The man gave her a small smile, one side of his mouth quirking up higher than the other again in that crooked smirk. She realized that he had a little dimple in his cheek that came out when he smiled. She wondered what it would be like to stick her tongue in the divot, then mentally shook herself. What the hell was wrong with her, lusting after her daughter's uncle? Sure, she felt an immediate attraction to him, but that didn't mean she needed to pay attention to that.

Plus the guy had come here under false pretenses, even though his motives seemed pure.

"My niece has been wanting to find her birth parents for several years now, but she had to wait until after she turned twenty-one to start the process. As I said, she got your information from the adoption agency, and I understand that she's going to make contact with you soon. I know I'm overreaching here Ms. Langdon, but if you don't want to meet her, if you're going to break her heart, I wanted to be prepared for that."

"You're close with my...um, with your niece?" Emily asked curiously.

"Yes. I'm her godfather and I've never had kids of my own, so we've always been close. Her parents, my sister and her husband, were killed in a car accident when she was fourteen. As her only living relative, I petitioned the courts for custody, and she moved in with me after they died."

"Her parents died?" Her hand went to her mouth. "That's terrible. I had no idea, obviously. Does she still live with you?" Emily asked.

Brian shook his head. "No, not anymore. She moved out on her own after she graduated from college and got a job. She rents an apartment in Logan Square with some roommates."

Emily leaned forward and met the man's gaze. "Mr. McKenna..."

"Brian, please."

"Brian. The agency notified me that Jane had asked for her records to be unsealed, so ever since then I've been expecting to hear from her. You don't have to worry. I agreed to be contacted by her twenty-one years ago and I haven't changed my mind. In fact, I'm eager to meet her and hear about her life. I won't blow her off. If the situations were reversed I would want to at least meet my mother and get some answers about where I came from."

Brian exhaled loudly. "Oh great. Thank you. I'm so glad to hear that. I really appreciate you talking to me, and I apologize again for the subterfuge."

"As long as you're here, can you tell me a little about her?" she asked, her voice suddenly small and unsure. "I, uh, well they didn't give me any information other than her full name and that she might be contacting me. It's made me curious about her."

"Jane is an incredible young woman," he said proudly. "She was a happy child. She got good grades, participated in sports, and she had a wide circle of friends. And she's super smart. I'm guessing she takes after her bio mom there. She went to Northwestern and studied finance, then landed a job at Mead & Lowe right out of college."

Her eyes widened at the mention of the largest investment firm in Chicago. "Wow. That's impressive. Did her parents have other children?"

Brian shook his head. "She was an only child. I think that's part of why she's been so eager to meet her biological family. Can I ask, she told me that her birth certificate says the father was unknown. Are you still..."?

Emily interrupted his question. "It's a long story that I think I should tell Jane first out of respect for her. But to answer your question, no I'm not in contact with the father."

"Does she have other family?" he asked. "Siblings? Grandparents? Cousins? I'm afraid that I'm all the family she has right now."

"I, um, that's a bit of a complicated story as well, and again I would prefer to tell Jane first."

He nodded, looking at her curiously. She knew he was wondering what the story was but respected her wishes to tell her daughter directly. She appreciated that. He was clearly very protective of her daughter, and it must be hard for him to sit with all the unknowns.

"I understand. I'll get out of your hair now Emily. Thank you so much for your time."

He stood up to leave and she followed him to the door, reaching out to shake his hand again out of habit. Their eyes met at the same time as their palms, and for a long moment they stood there staring at each other. She saw his eyes darken and his pupils dilate at the same time her heartrate started racing. The air around them felt suddenly heavy as attraction arced between them.

It really was too bad this guy was her daughter's uncle. She hadn't been this attracted to a guy in a long, long time. She hadn't dated anyone in a while. Maybe...no, this was her daughter's uncle.

She broke the contact regretfully. "Goodbye Brian. I'm glad Jane has you looking out for her."

He gave her a long look and left without another word. Emily's legs were shaky as she returned to her desk and sank into her chair. She pressed her hand against her chest, willing her heart rate to slow down.

Was she really going to go through with this? Was she going to meet this girl and tell her everything that had happened? She wasn't sure how prepared Jane would be for the emotional fallout of this decision. She wasn't sure how prepared she was herself to have this discussion.

Emily had come to terms with her decision years ago, knowing that she'd made the best decision for her daughter, and herself. Years of counseling had helped her move past the trauma of getting pregnant the way she had and giving up her child for adoption. Time had dulled some of the pain of her loss, but now it all seemed to be rushing back.

In some ways she'd never recovered from what happened. Emily had never gotten married and didn't have any other children. She knew she owed it to herself and her daughter to at least meet Jane, even if they didn't decide to have a relationship. She couldn't bear to reject her daughter; she understood all too well the devastation of being rejected by your parents. Jane deserved answers, even if they were hard to hear.

Emily was also intensely curious about her daughter. She'd thought of her often over the years, hoping she was doing OK, and wondering what she was like. Even if she only got to see her once, it would be worth it. Based on what Brian had told her, Jane had been loved and well cared for and had turned into a successful adult. She smiled to herself, knowing that her sacrifice had been worth it.

Almost as if thinking about her summoned her, Emily opened up her email and saw an email from a Jane Scott.

Dear Emily Langdon,

My name is Jane Marie Scott, and I have been informed by the Sisters of Harmony adoption program that I am your daughter. I was born on June 15, 1999, at Mercy Hospital. Hopefully the adoption agency has notified you by now that my records have been unsealed and that I requested information on my birth parents. I would really like to meet you and hope you feel the same. Could we meet for dinner or something some time? We both live in the Chicagoland area, and I am happy to meet you anytime, anywhere, at your convenience. I hope to hear from you soon. You can email me at the address above or call me at 312-555-1122.

Sincerely, Jane Scott

Emily read through the email several times. She wondered if her daughter had agonized over the wording of the email, the way she would have done if the situation was reversed.

Of course she would meet her daughter, but she wondered when and where would be best. They would need to have a difficult conversation, one Emily wasn't looking forward to, but it was necessary. Should she invite Jane to her house? Propose a quiet restaurant somewhere? What if the girl started to cry when she heard the news? What if Emily did? It's not like there was a guidebook for this kind of thing.

She debated waiting for a while to respond, but imagined that her daughter would be on pins and needles waiting to see if she replied. She knew it took courage for Jane to put herself out there like this. She re-opened her email and composed a response. No sense procrastinating.

Brian

"Uncle Brian? Are you here?"

"In the kitchen." Brian looked up as his niece rushed in, her blue eyes sparkling with excitement.

"Guess what?"

Before he could answer, she continued in a rush, "I emailed my birth mother Emily, and she already wrote back, and she seems really cool, and she wants to meet me, and we just need to figure out when and where."

Brian nodded towards the dish he was taking out of the oven. "That's awesome. Are you hungry?" he asked. "I made some chicken."

"Yeah that would be great," Jane said. Without being prompted, she moved around the kitchen setting the table and pouring two glasses of water. Brian brought the chicken, potatoes, and vegetables he'd cooked to the table. He'd made extra, thinking he would bring the rest to work for lunch tomorrow, but he could share with Jane instead.

"Tell me more."

Jane smiled as she served herself a plate of food.

"Well, I dithered for a while about what to so, but I finally emailed her yesterday afternoon. She responded almost right away, and we exchanged a few emails back and forth last night and today, getting to know each other a bit. I told her that there's no pressure if she doesn't want to have a relationship, but I would really like to at least meet her once. She told me it's up to me. She said she really wanted to meet me too, but that she wanted to let me drive the process, which I thought was really nice."

"That is nice. What's the plan?" he asked.

It looked like his visit to Emily hadn't been needed, but he was glad he'd gone anyway. Even if he couldn't stop thinking about the blue-eyed beauty.

Jane frowned. "I definitely want to meet her soon, like maybe this weekend. She suggested that we meet at either her house or someplace private to talk instead of being in public. Then I asked her about my father, my birth father that is, and she said she preferred to talk about that in person. Then I asked her some other questions about her family, and she said the same thing."

Brian chewed his chicken and had a flash of worry. He had a bad feeling this was not going to be a good story.

"Jane, I just want to make sure that you're mentally prepared for this. You might meet your birth mother and not like each other. Or you might hear some things from her about your other family members that aren't good. Not everyone had the good home life and loving family that you did."

She nodded in acknowledgement. "The thing is Uncle Brian, from her response to my questions about my father and the other family members, I'm assuming it's something that will be hard to hear. There's a reason she wants to avoid meeting in public. It's not like people who are in happy, committed relationships give their kids up for adoption."

"What are you going to do?"

"She gave me the option to come over to her house tomorrow afternoon if I was ready that soon. I think I'm going to take her up on that. Only...."

He raised his eyebrows. "Only what?"

"Do you think it would be weird if I brought you with me?" she asked, suddenly looking very young. "I don't want her to think I'm immature or something, but I would feel better if you were there with me, especially if it's bad news. I might need some support."

"I'm glad to go with you, if that's what you want," Brian reassured her. "I'm sure Emily would be fine with it."

Jane slid her phone out of her pocket. "Oh great, thanks a lot Uncle Brian, that means a lot to me to have you there for support. She gave me her phone number. I'm going to text her right now to confirm for tomorrow."

The next day he and Jane drove up to Evanston to meet Emily. He'd never seen his niece so nervous. She scarcely said a word in the car, which was not like her.

Jane's birth mother lived in a brick townhouse on a street dotted with thick trees and green patches of grass. It looked like a nice upper middle class neighborhood, but not as fancy as he'd expected someone as successful as Emily would live. After seeing her office, he expected her to live in some high price condo in a fancy neighborhood.

They found a parking spot not too far and walked up the stairs to the navy blue door. Jane was trembling with nervousness next to him, and he reached out to squeeze her hand reassuringly before he rang the doorbell.

The door opened immediately, as if Emily had been hovering by the door waiting for them to arrive. He eyed her hungrily. Ever since he met her the other day she'd been in his thoughts pretty much non-stop. He'd spent more time than he wanted to admit replaying their conversation and wondering about the strange pull he'd felt between them. It was too bad she was his niece's birth mother, if he'd met her under other circumstances he would be inclined to ask her out and explore their attraction.

Emily was dressed casually today in faded jeans that lovingly hugged her slim curves, and a blue shirt that brought out the color in her eyes. He glanced down and hid a smile as he saw that she was wearing socks with little cartoon kittens on them. He wouldn't have pegged her for a whimsical sock person.

"Jane, hello." Emily's voice was soft, her eyes shiny as she eyed her daughter. "I'm so glad you came."

"Hi, um," Jane stopped and laughed awkwardly. "I'm not sure what I should call you."

"Emily is fine," her mother reassured her.

Her eyes moved to Brian, and he felt that jolt of connection again. "This is my Uncle Brian," Jane told her. "He's the one I told you about."

"Nice to meet you Brian," Emily said, her voice neutral.

Brian shot her a look of gratitude for ignoring their previous meeting. He had a feeling that Jane would be annoyed if she knew that he'd meddled on her behalf. He reached his hand out to shake Emily's hand and as their palms met he felt that same electrical current of awareness passing through him. The overwhelming attraction that he felt when he'd visited her office wasn't a fluke. He knew from her widened eyes that she felt it too. She pulled her hand away quickly, and a slight flush rose on her pale cheeks.

"Both of you, please come in."

They followed her into a comfortable looking living room. A dark blue overstuffed couch faced a brick fireplace, flanked with built in shelves that were painted an antique white. Matching armchairs were placed on either side of the couch, making a nice conversational seating area. Dark brown baseboards and crown molding offset the white of the walls. The hardwood floors were stained the same color as the moldings, but broken up a with colorful rugs in shades of blue and red.

"What can I get you to drink?" Emily asked. "I have water, coke, diet coke, beer, orange juice, wine, or ginger ale."

"I'll have diet coke please," Jane responded, wandering around the room curiously.

"Just water for me, please," Brian added.

"I'll be right back," Emily promised. "Make yourself comfortable."

Brian settled on one side of the couch as Jane looked around the space. She was examining some framed pictures on the mantel when Emily returned with a tray of drinks and a plate of cookies. She set everything on the coffee table and glanced over at the picture in her daughter's hand.

"That's me with my friends Amber and Jenny at our high school graduation," she told Jane with a fond smile. "We've been best friends since the first week of high school, and we all went to college together. We still talk almost every day."

"That's so cool." Jane sat next to him on the couch, her nervousness palpable.

Emily placed their drinks in front of each of them on a coaster, then angled one of the chairs on the side to face them. He and Jane both took a sip of their drinks and the silence lengthened. Emily caught his gaze, then looked away again and fixed her gaze on his niece.

"Jane I appreciate you reaching out to me," Emily began. "I always wondered if I would hear from you some day. I know that it took a lot of courage to put yourself out there like. I also want to say that I was so sorry to hear the news when you emailed me about losing your parents. That must have been really hard. I'm just glad you had your uncle to take care of you when it happened."

Jane nodded and reached over to squeeze Brian's hand. "Yeah, he's pretty great."

"I'm excited for us to get to know each other," Emily continued, "And I know you have a lot of questions for me but if it's OK, I'd like to start with the story of how I got pregnant, and what happened after. I think it's important for you to know why I gave you up for adoption before you make the decision to move forward in spending time with me."

Jane nodded. "Sure, I'd appreciate hearing everything that you can share with me."

She took a deep breath and her gaze skittered back to Brian for a moment before returning to her daughter.

"I just want to warn you that it's not a happy story, and I haven't talked really about it with anyone since it happened, other than with my therapist. It's, um, super traumatic for me, and I know that it will be hard for you to hear it. You deserve to hear the truth, but I want to make sure you're really ready to deal with it."

Brian's heart dropped. He'd had a feeling something bad was coming, and based on the pale, stricken look on Emily's face and the way her voice had taken on a robotic tone, he knew that none of them was going to like what she had to share.

Emily

"I'm ready Emily, if you are."

Emily stared at her daughter's eyes, a mirror image of her own. Looking at Jane was like looking at herself twenty years ago. Even she could see the strong resemblance between them. In fact, as she searched her daughter's face, she couldn't see even a hint of her father, the face that had haunted her nightmares for so many years. She was grateful for that.

She glanced over at Brian. His grim face told her that he was prepared for the worst. His instinct was correct. There was no easy way to do this, she just needed to get it out. Her stomach burned with acid.

"The first thing I want to tell you is that I loved you Jane, I loved you very much. I loved you from the minute I knew you were inside me. Giving you up for adoption was the second hardest thing that I ever experienced, but I wanted you to have the best life possible, and I knew in my heart that it wouldn't be with me. It almost killed me to separate from you, but I did it for you, I promise."

Jane nodded, looking apprehensive, and Emily took a deep breath, willing her heart rate to slow.

"I got pregnant with you my senior year of college, down at U of I," she began, her voice steady and emotionless. "I was at a frat party, and I got pretty drunk. You know how it is at some of these college parties, I'm sure, with everyone drinking more than they should."

Jane nodded.

"There was this guy at the party who came up to me and started flirting with me. He was really cute and charming, and before I knew it, we were doing shots of Jaeger together. I didn't really know who he was, I'd never seen him around campus before. He said his name was Mark and he claimed to go to Iowa State. He said that he was in Urbana visiting friends from high school, but I don't know if it was even true."

Emily could tell from the look on Jane's face that her daughter had a feeling where this story was going. She was a smart girl, and she likely had friends with similar experiences. Emily just hoped like hell that Jane didn't have firsthand experience with what happened.

"Mark asked me to go for a drive with him. We were both starving, and he suggested we go to Taco Bell since they were open all night. Like an idiot, I agreed, even though I knew he was really drunk. I just took off with him. I didn't even tell my friends where I was going, I just disappeared."

She still couldn't believe that she'd gotten into a car with a drunken stranger like that. She should have known better; she would have known better if she hadn't been so damn drunk. But it wasn't like she could change the past.

"We drove for a while, then he stopped at a picnic area instead of going into town. We got out at the forest preserve and we were, um, making out for a while and I was OK with that. Enjoyed it even. But then he started pressuring me for...more. I tried to put the brakes on it, told him I didn't want to, but he got angry and called me a tease. And then he got...aggressive."

"He forced you?" Brian bit out, sounding angry.

She nodded and took another deep breath, willing herself not to hyperventilate. *Stay detached Emily,* she reminded herself. *Protect yourself.*

"I tried to fight, that's what they tell you to do, but he was much stronger than me. I scratched him and then punched me in the face pretty hard, and I fell backwards. I think my head hit the picnic table or something because I blacked out. When I, um, when I woke up some time later I was all alone. I had a bruise on my cheek and a bump on the back of my head. My clothes were ripped to shreds. I didn't remember what happened, but I could tell that...well, I could tell what happened. I could *feel* what happened."

"Oh my god!" Jane gasped.

"That was before we had cell phones of course so I couldn't call anyone. Finally, I just walked to the road and hitchhiked back to campus."

"Did you call the police?" Jane asked. Her eyes were shiny and red like she was trying not to cry.

Emily nodded. "I didn't want to at first. I was so ashamed about what happened, but my friends insisted. But when the police came, they told me there was nothing they could do. I only had his first name, I couldn't describe his car, and I didn't even remember exactly what had happened. By the time my friends had convinced me to talk to the cops it was the next day. I had already showered like fifteen times, so it was too late to get a...um, to get a rape kit done."

She met her daughter's eyes. "I'm sure you know that the system doesn't support women who are assaulted, and it was much worse back then. The cops acted like I was some dumb girl who was asking for it. One guy even insinuated that I was just trying to cause trouble because I changed my mind after agreeing to have sex."

Tears were running down Jane's face now, her eyes rimmed with red. Emily reminded herself to stay detached. She embraced the numbness to protect herself.

"I told myself I should just try to forget it and put it all behind me, but a few weeks later I realized I was pregnant. I hadn't been with anyone else in months, so I knew I'd gotten pregnant that night. It wasn't like I could tell him since I had no idea who the guy really was or how to find him. I never saw him again."

Thank god, she added silently.

Emily could feel the nausea rising in her as she remembered that horrible day she'd realized that she was pregnant. She'd been terrified. Amber and Jenny had insisted that she take multiple pregnancy tests just to be sure, but she'd known she was pregnant even before the tests confirmed it.

"I'd made an appointment at the clinic, but I couldn't bring myself to go through with the abortion," she continued. ". I went home for Thanksgiving and told my parents that I was pregnant. I told them that I'd been raped."

She dug her fingers into her thigh to ground herself and took a slow breath in before exhaling through her nose, the way her therapist had taught her so long ago, fighting not to break down in front of them.

Brian put his arm around Jane, offering her silent comfort as if he knew there was still more to the story.

"My parents, they were very conservative and religious. They got angry and said they didn't believe I was attacked. They told me I brought it on myself with the way I dressed, the way I acted, the way I'd gone off with a stranger. They said God was punishing me for my sins and that I got what I deserved, and that they were ashamed to have a whore for a daughter. Then they told me to get out of their house, that they never wanted to see me or my bastard child again."

Jane gasped, her expression shocked. Emily's gaze shot over to Brian. He looked like he was going to punch something, his face flushed with anger. She appreciated that they believed her, that they shared her horror over what had happened. She hadn't known how much she needed their understanding until just now.

"I never talked to my parents again, and we really didn't have other family for me to rely on. But I had Jenny and Amber. I went back to college, finished my last semester while pregnant with you, and you were born shortly after graduation. I agonized about keeping you, but I didn't have a job yet and wasn't sure how I was going to support myself let alone take care of a child."

She met Jane's gaze and added, "I have to be honest with you Jane. I was also worried that every time I saw you, it would remind me about what happened. I worried that it would impact my ability to be a good parent for you, if I would be able to love you if you looked like...him. I only wanted the best for you, so I decided to give you a chance at a better life with parents who could be what you needed. After you were born, I held you in my arms for a few minutes, then the nuns came to take you to your adoptive parents, and I kissed you goodbye. I was devastated, but I never forgot you. I never stopped thinking about you."

She stood up and handed Jane a picture she'd kept hidden in a box all these years. "My friends took this picture of us together before I said goodbye to you."

Brian and Jane looked at the photo, slightly curled at the edges. It showed a girl who looked just like Jane, tears running down her cheeks while she held a sleeping baby wrapped in a pink blanket. The baby looked like a little angel. Emily had stared at the photo a million times over the years, praying that she'd done the right thing.

The room was quiet for a long time other than the soft sounds of Jane sniffing. Her daughter finally stood up and walked over to her. Emily stood up uncertainly and was surprised when Jane pulled her close in a tight hug. Emily gathered her daughter into her arms for the first time since the picture had been taken twenty-one years ago, and something inside her healed.

"Thank you Emily," Jane gasped as she squeezed her almost painfully tight. Emily could feel the dampness of her daughter's tears on her shoulder. "Thank you for what you did for me, and thank you for telling me the truth even though it was hard to hear. It means a lot to me."

They stood like that for a long time before they reluctantly broke apart. Jane wiped her tears and asked with a shaky voice, "What happens now?"

Emily met her gaze. "It's up to you Jane. I would love the opportunity to get to know you better and spend some time with you. Develop a relationship. But I know this is all a lot, maybe too much to think about. Do you need some time?"

Jane nodded. "I think I do need some time to process. If it's OK with you I think I'll go home for now and take some time to think about what you told me. Can I talk to you later?"

"Of course. Take all the time you need. And I want you to know that I'll totally understand if this is all too much to take in, if you don't want to talk again."

"Everything I've heard today just makes me want to get to know you even more, Emily."

A sense of relief rushed through her.

Brian got up and stood by his niece, his eyes soft and kind as they met hers. She felt drained and numb and somehow those warm brown eyes felt like a lifeline. It made no sense given this was only the second time they'd met, but Emily appreciated it regardless. It was all she could do not to throw herself into his arms and take comfort from him.

"Are you ready to go, pumpkin?" Brian asked quietly, putting a hand on Jane's shoulder.

Her daughter nodded, stepping close to give her another hug. Emily had never been much of a hugger. Her parents certainly weren't the warm and fuzzy type so there wasn't a lot affection in her home growing up, but still, she appreciated Jane's strong embrace. Her parents had raised her to be open about her emotions and to show affection, and it made her doubly glad that Jane had them in her life, at least a little while.

"I'll talk to you soon Emily," Jane promised.

"Whenever you're ready, I'm here for you."

Emily watched from the window as they drove off, then collapsed to the floor, staring into space until the darkness fell.

Brian

"Are you OK, Pumpkin?"

Jane had been quiet the entire drive back to her place. Brian pulled into a parking space across the street from her apartment, sparing a thought for what a miracle it was that he'd just found a spot so close, and turned off the car, turning to face his niece.

"Yeah, it's just a lot, you know?" she responded. "I think I had it in my head that my parents were like high school sweethearts or something, I never imagined that my father was a...," she paused and took a deep breath, "a rapist."

He nodded but didn't respond. What could he say anyway? The news was shocking to both of them.

"Poor Emily, I can't believe she went through that," Jane continued. "One of my good friends was assaulted at a party in high school and well, she's never been the same since then. After it happened, I remember us all saying how grateful we were that he hadn't gotten her pregnant. I can't even imagine how much worse it would have been if she'd had to deal with a pregnancy too."

"At least you know the truth now, as terrible as it is," he stated. "What are you going to do now?"

"I think I'm going to just take the weekend to process this," Jane said. "But I definitely want to see Emily again and get to know her. Especially after hearing what happened. I can't believe her parents were such assholes. I mean, how do you treat your daughter like that?"

That had been one of the most shocking parts of the story. As horrible as it was that Emily had been violated that way, knowing that her parents had blamed her for the attack – it was unfathomable. He was tempted to find out where they lived and go beat the shit out of them.

He flashed on Emily's rigid control as she told them the story and his heart wrenched in his chest. Somehow he knew she'd been hanging on by a thread. He'd wanted so much to pull her into his arms and tell her that she'd never have to go through anything alone again, which was a ridiculous impulse given that they scarcely knew each other.

"Do you think she's OK, Uncle Brian? I mean, after sharing all that? As hard as it was to hear, it had to be worse to relive it. I could tell she was trying to be strong in front of us, but she looked ready to shatter."

He nodded. "I'm sure she's fine, or as fine as anyone could be after having to tell her daughter that story. But if you want to give me her number, I'm glad to check on her later if you'd like. She might feel less inclined to put on a brave face with someone her own age."

He tried not to be happy that he now had an excuse to contact her, given the circumstances. He knew it made him an asshole, but he was fascinated by her. There was a part of him that kept whispering in his mind that she was what he'd been missing all these years.

"That would be great Uncle Brian." Jane fiddled with her phone, then he heard his own phone beep. "I just sent you her contact info."

She leaned across and gave him a hug, then pulled back and gave him a considering look.

"Did you like Emily?"

"She seems nice," he answered mildly, wondering at the change in her tone.

His niece studied him carefully. "I thought I felt a vibe between you two."

"A vibe?" he asked innocently.

Jane shook her head. "You know what I mean. That long handshake with the staring in the foyer. The way your eyes kept meeting when we were talking. There was definitely some heat between you. Just so you know, I would be fine with it if you wanted to ask her out or something. I mean, you're both single."

"Today's probably not the best time to talk about this, with everything that happened."

When in doubt, go for the redirect, he thought.

Jane nodded. "You're right. Thanks again for coming along with me, and for driving." She leaned over and gave him a quick hug. "I'll talk to you later."

He waited until early evening before reaching out to Emily. He tried to tell himself that he was just being nice, checking on her after such a traumatic conversation. But he knew it was more than that. He couldn't stop thinking about her, and not just because he was worried about how she was doing after sharing what she shared with them.

Brian: *Hi Emily, it's Brian. I hope you don't mind, but Jane gave me your number.*

Emily: *How is Jane? Is she OK? I know that was hard for her to hear. I wouldn't blame her if she wanted to just forget this whole thing.*

Brian: *I just talked to her. She's a little shell-shocked but she's doing OK and hoping to talk to you again soon. I promised her I would check on you and see how you're doing. I know you were trying to shield her a bit.*

Emily: *Oh, that was nice of you. It felt a little cathartic, actually. I'd visualized for years how that conversation would go if Jane decided to contact me. And honestly, I debated not telling her, glossing over the truth and just saying it was a one-night stand or something, but I didn't want to start our relationship off by being dishonest.*

Brian: *I know she'd want the truth, no matter how hard, so thanks for telling her.*

Emily: *I appreciate you checking on me. I'm sure I'll see you again some time. Good night.*

He debated for a few minutes about continuing the conversation after she'd not so subtly dismissed him. Ultimately he decided not to, but he knew he was going to have to see her again. He couldn't explain it, but he knew that he needed to get to know her better. After obsessing about her like a lovesick teenager, he decided to reach out again the next evening.

Brian: *How was the rest of your weekend?*

Emily: *It was OK. Pretty chill. How about yours?*

Brian: *Same. I just talked to Jane btw, she's doing fine.*

Emily: *Yeah, she texted me earlier, but thanks for letting me know.*

Brian: *Would you be interested in coming over for dinner sometime this week? I make a great lasagna.*

Emily: *...*

Brian watched the dots disappear and reappear several times as she composed her answer. He hoped she didn't think he was a creep.

Emily: *With Jane you mean?*

Brian: *Yes, I asked her and she's free Tuesday or Thursday night if either of those work for you. I know she wants to have the "get to know you" conversation that you couldn't have yesterday.*

Emily: *Oh, OK yes. Sorry, for a minute there I thought you were asking me out, LOL. Thursday works. Let me know what time, and your address.*

Brian: *What if I was?*

Emily: *Huh?*

Brian: *What if I was asking you out? What would you say?*

Emily: *I would say that we don't know each other and that I'd be worried that it would be weird for Jane.*

Brian: *She already told me she was fine with it if I decided to ask you out. She said we have a "vibe".*

Emily: *...*

She took so long to respond that he became nervous that he'd totally freaked her out. He decided to put his cards on the table.

Brian: *I'm sorry if I made this weird. I feel like there's a connection between us, and that doesn't happen often, at least for me. I would regret it if I didn't at least ask you, even if the timing isn't perfect. You're not dating anyone, right? Jane said you were single.*

Emily: *...*

Emily: *How about we try being friends first? I want to focus on getting to know my daughter without making things any more complicated than they already are.*

Brian: *OK I can live with that. For now. See you around 6:30 on Thursday night.*

Emily

Emily exited the "El" station – Chicago's elevated train – and walked the two blocks to Brian's house. She'd worked in the office today and come straight over when she'd finished for the day, so she was still wearing the dress she'd worn to work.

She'd chosen it on purpose, although she would deny it if anyone asked. The jade green dress was one of her most flattering work-appropriate dresses, the kind of dress that could easily go from the office to a nighttime social activity. The fact that it highlighted both her complexion and her figure was just a bonus.

The last few days had been weird, to say the least. She had talked to Brian via text every day since Saturday. First he was just checking on her after their hard conversation, but then they both kept the chat going. They seemed to be developing a friendship over text, and their messages were gradually getting longer and more personal as they got to know each other.

Even when they weren't texting, Brian wasn't far from her mind. As much as she chastised herself for having a schoolgirl crush on her daughter's uncle, she still couldn't help the smile on her face when her phone beeped and she saw a message from him. And if he happened to invade her dreams at night...well, she wasn't going to share that tidbit with anyone else.

Meanwhile she'd also been talking to Jane several times a day, mostly lighthearted tidbits about their day. Between the two of them, she had texted more in the last week than she had texted with anyone in the last year, even Amber and Jenny.

Emily walked up to a large brick building and checked the address. As was typical in many Chicago neighborhoods, the building was "U" shaped, with three floors of condos and apartments surrounding the central courtyard area. The courtyard area was filled with gardening boxes, giving the whole area a homey vibe.

Brian lived on the top floor at the end of one building. She passed the elevator and took the stairs. She was in her forties now and she was trying to incorporate more exercise in her daily life in addition to the running and yoga she did on a regular basis.

Jane opened the door as soon as she knocked. "Emily! Come in!" Her daughter pulled her in for a quick hug. "We're just finishing up dinner."

She had quick impression of a comfortable living room with a fireplace and a leather couch as she followed Jane to the kitchen. Brian stood at the counter making a salad. Both he and Jane had changed into casual clothes, wearing jeans and t-shirts, and walking around in bare feet. They worked together as if their work was choreographed, telling her that they'd been doing this for years. It was very homey, and for a minute she almost felt like an intruder.

She'd never had "homey" when she was growing up. Her family's meals were full of angry silences and laden with disappointment.

"Emily, welcome," Brian gave her a big smile and she felt herself relaxing. "We just opened some Riesling. Would you like a glass? Or I also have water, beer, or coke."

"Wine is fine, thanks."

She handed him a bakery box tied with a string. "I picked up a cinnamon babka for dessert." Despite her afore-mentioned desire to keep in shape, Emily had a weakness for the cake-like dessert.

"Nice. Thank you," Brian replied.

"Cinnamon babka? That's my favorite!" Jane exclaimed. Another thing they had in common.

Emily offered to help with dinner, but Brian and Jane insisted that she sit down and keep them company instead. Emily looked around the comfortable kitchen. The cabinets and appliances were older but well maintained. The floor was old school linoleum that had likely been there for years. Everything was meticulously clean, making her wonder if Brian was a neat freak or if he used a cleaning service.

The three of them chatted easily until Brian informed them that the lasagna was done, then they moved into the dining room. There was a small round table with seating for four in the room, as well as built in shelves that were filled with serving dishes, pictures, and other mementos.

She looked at the framed photos on the shelf, stopping to pick up a picture of a happy looking young couple holding a baby.

"Are these your parents?" she asked.

"Yes," Jane said with a fond smile.

"Did you live here after your folks died?" she asked Jane.

"Yeah. I moved in with Uncle Brian after we sold my parents' house in the suburbs."

Emily picked up another picture of a younger Brian with his arms around a little blonde girl in pigtails. Jane looked like she was about five in the picture. They were standing in front of Wrigley Field, decked out in Cubs gear. They were adorable and she felt her heart swell with affection.

"Let's eat."

Emily sat next to Brian and across from Jane. Brian served them each a generous slice of lasagna, then passed around the salad and some freshly sliced bread. As he handed her the basket of bread, their fingers touched. They both stopped, staring at each other for a long moment as a rush of awareness flew through her body, settling at her core. She felt her breath catch and everything in her stilled. Everything around them faded away as the moment stretched between them.

Jane cleared her throat, breaking the spell, and she moved her hand back quickly as if she'd been burned. She could feel Brian's gaze on her but stared down at her plate. What was it about this guy? And why did he seem so familiar? If she believed in that kind of thing, she would swear that they'd met in another life or something.

Jane looked between them, amusement lighting her eyes. "You know Emily, Uncle Brian is single. And I know that you're single..."

"Jane!" Brian's tone held a warning.

Jane raised her eyebrows. "Just making conversation," she said with false innocence.

"How about we talk about your love life then, young lady?" Brian rejoined.

Jane sat back. "Fine, I'll change the subject. How about those Cubs?"

"Good lord Brian, this lasagna is delicious," Emily exclaimed, ignoring the interchange between Jane and her uncle.

He shot her a pleased smile. "Thanks, it was my mom's recipe."

"Uncle Brian is a really good cook, and an all-around great guy."

Brian raised one eyebrow at her in warning, and Jane lapsed into silence, focusing on her food.

The rest of the meal passed quickly, with easy conversation flowing between the three of them. Jane peppered Emily with questions about her experiences in high school and college, about her job, and about her friends. Emily gamely answered every question and encouraged Jane to tell her more about her own experiences growing up.

Brian was mostly silent, listening to them as they connected and shared their stories. It felt very comfortable, and Emily felt herself relax more around them as the night went on. It made her happy to feel the immediate connection between them and she was relieved that Jane didn't seem to have any judgement around the circumstances of her conception. She'd heard enough adoption reunion horror stories to know that it didn't always go this well.

Emily was also fascinated to see that she and her daughter had so many things in common despite being separated all those years. They not only looked alike, but they also had many similar interests and experiences. They even shared the trait of chewing on their lower lip when they were nervous. It was uncanny.

When they'd finished eating Jane and Brian cleared the table and loaded the dishwasher, once again refusing her offer of help. They returned with coffee and the babka box. Brian waved the box in front of her.

"Do you want a slice of babka, Emily?"

Their eyes met for a beat.

"Yes please, just a small one."

Brian had just started cutting the cake when Jane suddenly stood up, looking at her bare wrist as if there were a watch there.

"Oh damn, I forgot I need to be somewhere now," she said with a mischievous smile. "Thanks for dinner Uncle Brian. Nice to see you again Emily, I'll talk to you soon."

Giving them each a quick hug, she raced out of the apartment before either of them could respond. As they heard the door slam behind her, Brian looked at her with a laugh. "Well, that was subtle."

"Yeah. I think someone's playing matchmaker," Emily laughed, shaking her head. "Well, thanks for dinner, but I think I should get going now."

She stood up and started to move away, but she stopped as Brian's hand shot out and grabbed her wrist. Emily gasped as his warm fingers circled the smooth skin loosely, just enough to forestall her movement.

"Please stay." He rose to stand in front of her. "You didn't get any babka yet. You can't say no to babka."

He shot her that crooked smirk that she loved, and she felt her panties dampen. She stood there frozen. It was hard to think with Brian's fingers circling her wrist. Had she ever been this inexplicably attracted to a guy? If so, she didn't remember. It was like she was a teenager with a crush, but the feelings were much more intense.

They stared at each other for a long time, as if they were in a trance, until Brian gave her wrist a tug, bringing her closer to him. She went easily, moving until she was less than an inch away from him. Brian gave her plenty of time to protest before he lowered his mouth to meet hers.

She gasped as their lips met, and Brian immediately took advantage, sweeping his tongue into her mouth. His kiss was hot and demanding and confident. She moved closer, wrapping her arms around his waist as one of his hands rose to cup the back of her head, fingers threading through the fine stands of her blonde hair.

Her nipples hardened against his chest and Brian growled into her mouth as if he could feel it. His other hand slid down to her butt, gripping her and pulling her even closer until they were pressed against each other. She could feel his erection growing against her stomach. It felt impressive.

They kissed until they were both out of breath, then stepped apart, as if by mutual agreement.

Emily fell back into her chair, wondering what in the hell had just happened. Her heart was beating so hard she was sure it was going to jump right out of her chest. Brian's eyes were dark with arousal, breath ragged, and it took everything she had not to leap into his lap and start riding him.

"That was...," she paused, unable to find a word to describe what she was feeling.

"Yeah," he acknowledged. He didn't need to say anything else.

She was forty-three years old, and she had certainly kissed her fair share of men over the years. But this, this was like no other kiss she remembered. It was all-consuming. Had she ever been so flummoxed by a simple kiss before? Not that anything about that kiss was simple. It was the benchmark by which she'd measure all future kisses.

And for some strange reason, as he had held her in his arms, she felt inexplicably comfortable, like she was coming home. Something about Brian made her feel safe, and that freaked her out more than anything.

What the hell was she thinking? Everything about this was complicated. Brian was her newly-found daughter's uncle and guardian. She didn't want to do anything to alienate her daughter now that they'd finally found each other. Despite Jane's obvious matchmaking, this situation could very easily blow up in all of their faces.

As if sensing her discomfort, Brian looked away and busied himself slicing up the babka. He slid a plate towards her before serving himself a piece. She took a large gulp of her wine. They ate quietly for a few minutes before Brian finally broke the silence.

"I feel like I should apologize to you, but I'm not actually sorry," he began.

She looked up at him curiously.

"I know it's weird the way we met, and with the connection we both have to Jane this has the potential to be messy."

She nodded and he continued, "We're too old to play games so I'm just going to put this out there. I like you Emily, and that kiss was incredible. I haven't been able to stop thinking about you since we met. I've never felt this way about anyone before, and I want us to explore whatever this is between us. To see what happens."

"I...I don't know Brian. I like you too, but I think I need time," she finally responded. "This is a lot to process. It feels like my life has completely turned upside down over the last two weeks. This really isn't the best time for me to think about dating. I should really go home now."

She waited to see if he would argue, then couldn't decide if she was relieved or disappointed when he nodded, giving her a sad smile.

"Will you text me when you get home?" he asked. "Let me know you got home OK?"

She felt a little thrill. It had been a long time since anyone had wanted to take care of her, other than Amber and Jenny. It was kind of nice.

"I will."

As she walked back to the El station, she asked herself once again what the hell she was doing. She'd literally been through hell with her parents, with the attack, and giving up Jane for adoption. It had taken her years to move past all of that, and she had d promised herself two things all those years ago: she would never rely on anyone else again, and she would always protect her heart.

She had a bad feeling that Brian was going to destroy both of those vows.

Brian

It had been a few days since the dinner with Emily, but she was never far from Brian's mind. They talked every day on text, their conversations getting longer and more personal as they got to know each other better. He hadn't asked to see her again though. She was pretty guarded, almost skittish, and he wanted to give her space.

Today he was hanging out with Jane, and he was looking forward to seeing her again. Years ago, Brian and a couple of his friends had purchased two season tickets for the Cubs, and they rotated the tickets between them. With about eighty home games in a season, they all had ample opportunity to go to the games. Today was his turn, and he'd invited his nice to join him for the game against the Cardinals, one of their team's biggest rivals.

He smiled as his niece met him near the gate. She was decked out in a Cubs shirt, Cubs hat, Cubs earrings, Cubs shoes, and carrying a Cubs purse on her shoulder. No shortage of team spirit with that one. They'd been attending games together since she was old enough to know what was going on, and Jane was convinced that showing her team spirit helped the Cubs win.

Brian greeted her with a hug, and they headed through security. As always, he felt a surge of excitement as he entered the historic baseball stadium, one of the oldest in the country. He'd been coming to games here since he was a little boy and Wrigley Field felt like home to him. They went right to the concession line to pick up some snacks to take back to their seats, catching up as they waited for the line to move.

"How's it going with Emily?" he asked curiously. He'd heard from Emily that things were going well, but he wanted to hear Jane's perspective.

"It's going good," Jane responded. "We've been talking a lot and I feel really connected to her. It's like I've known her for longer than I have."

He also felt very connected to Emily, though he couldn't understand why. He smiled at his niece. "That's great. I'm so glad you're getting along."

"We even signed up for Saturday morning Zumba class together. It starts next week."

"The dance thing?"

"Yep. Have you two been talking?" Jane asked curiously. "The way you were eye-fucking each other at dinner last week, my god I needed a cold shower after I left."

"Hey!" he chided, both shocked and embarrassed by his niece's words, even if they were true.

"I call it like I see it Uncle Brian," she said with a smug smile. The people ahead of them moved away and they approached the bored looking man at the counter. "Now what will it be? Treats are on me today."

After Jane paid they headed to their seats, loaded down with beer and hot dogs. Brian remembered how excited Jane was earlier this summer when she'd turned twenty-one and had been able to have her first beer at Wrigley Field. Her first legal beer, anyway. He was under no illusion that she hadn't done her share of drinking in high school and college like any other kid, but she'd always been responsible about it. He'd lucked out with her. Despite losing her parents at an impressionable age, she'd always been very level-headed and mature.

It was a beautiful sunny day, not too hot, perfect for a baseball game. Their seats were on the third base line, giving them a perfect view of the field. They watched the players warming up while they ate their hot dogs.

"Delicious," Jane said as she licked some mustard off her finger. "I don't know why hot dogs taste better here, but they totally do. Next I think I'll get cotton candy."

Brian rolled his eyes. "Cotton candy? Now there's a surprise!"

Jane had gotten a bag of pink cotton candy at every single game they'd ever attended. Even though she was all grown up now, she still loved the kids' treat. At least she wouldn't be leaving the game with her face and hands sticky with colored sugar like always happened when she was a little kid. His sister used to give him hell about letting her eat so much sugar.

Jane took out her phone and he shook his head. Her generation was surgically attached to those damn things. Her thumbs flew over her phone at a rapid pace, then she gave a little squeal. Brian looked at her curiously.

"Oh my god! Emily is at this game too!" she exclaimed. "What a coincidence!"

She turned her phone screen towards him, and he squinted at the picture. Emily had been tagged in an Instagram post, standing with two other women at today's game, all wearing big smiles. With their backs to the field, he could see they were on the same side of the stadium as they were.

"I'm going to text her."

Jane's phone beeped a few seconds later, then she stood up and started waving frantically. Brian followed her gaze and saw Emily standing facing them and waving back from about ten rows down from them, on the opposite end of the section. The two women next to Emily craned their necks to look back at them.

"That's so weird," he said. "Forty thousand seats at Wrigley Field and Emily and her friends are sitting in our same section at the same game?"

Jane moved down the row towards the aisle. "I know, right? I'll be right back. I'm going to go say hi."

He watched Emily greet his niece with a hug, then introduce her to her companions, both of whom hugged Jane as well. They chatted for a few minutes until the National Anthem started. Jane stopped in the aisle, standing respectfully until it was done, then made her way back to Brian's seats.

"You're never going to believe this," Jane told him when she came back. She paused to watch the first pitch.

"Emily and her friends share season tickets just like us. There's probably been a hundred times we were at the game together sitting ten rows apart and didn't know. I can't believe it."

"That is crazy," he answered, wondering if that's why Emily had looked so familiar when he first met her in her office that day.

He'd probably seen her at games and been attracted to her. It was a good reminder that while it had been worth it, his love life had been mostly on hold for a long time while he focused on taking care of Jane.

"I got to meet Emily's two best friends, that's who she's sitting with," Jane told him. "They invited us to join them after the game for dinner. I told them we would, I hope that was OK since we were planning to go out for dinner anyway."

"I'll let you go ahead," he responded, not wanting to horn in on Jane's bonding with her mother.

"Emily specifically invited you," she told him. "They have reservations at Italian Village and while I was there her friend called to make sure that they could add two more seats to their table, so it's all arranged already. I hope you don't mind my accepting for both of us, but I know you love that place and besides, Emily's friends really seemed to want to meet you."

That information gave him pause. Did that mean that Emily had talked about him to her friends? He felt ridiculously happy about that thought.

A few hours later they made their way down the aisle, exuberant after watching the Cubs beat the Cardinals. They found the three friends waiting by the concession stand just outside the doors to their section. Emily greeted him with a smile that made his heart stutter like he was a teenager with a crush instead of a fully grown man.

"Hi Brian, I hear we've been seat neighbors all this time. That's a weird coincidence."

"It sure is," he agreed.

He nodded to Emily's friends. "Hi, I'm Brian, Jane's uncle."

The two women gave him a friendly welcome. Like his niece, the three women were basically decked out head to toe in Cubs gear, other than their jeans. It looked like they were as much diehard fans as he and his niece were. With their hair up and tucked into ball caps, Emily and Jane could almost pass for sisters instead of mother and daughter.

The group of them exited the stadium and joined the long line waiting for the elevated train. It was too crowded to do much more than stand there, smashed together like sardines.

"If we get separated, we'll meet you in front of the restaurant," Emily told them right as the crowd pushed her forward away from him. Really it was a miracle that someone didn't get crushed to death after a game as everyone tried to catch the El.

They all ended up on the same train but in different cars. They met back up on the platform and walked over to the restaurant in a group. The Italian Village was one of the oldest restaurants in the city, and a local favorite. The restaurant was decorated in an old European style that made them feel like they'd entered another world. He and Jane liked to come here for special occasions.

Since they had a reservation, their group was immediately ushered to a large booth in back of the restaurant. Emily slid in first, moving towards the wall.

"Go on in Uncle Brian," Jane encouraged with a smile. "You can sit next to Emily."

His niece was not exactly subtle about her matchmaking. He slid in next to Emily, with Jane on his other side, with Jenny and Amber sitting on the opposite side from them. Jane subtly nudged him over and he slid closer to Emily, their thighs aligning on the seat. He could feel the heat of their connection through the fabric of his jeans and his cock twitched in excitement, telling him it was going to be a long dinner.

The waiter came over and they ordered wine and a calamari appetizer to share while waiting for their orders. Despite eating at the game, Brian was hungry and he dug into his gnocchi with gusto. Jane had also ordered gnocchi, but the other three went with seafood ravioli. Paired with fresh baked bread, the food was delicious.

Ninety minutes later, Brian had to admit that he was glad he'd came with the girls. He was stuffed with delicious food, and he'd sincerely enjoyed the company.

Emily and her friends regaled them with stories from their long friendship, while inserting questions directed towards Jane to involve her in the conversation. His niece seemed to fit right in with the group of old friends. It was amazing that they had all remained friends for so long; that didn't happen too often.

It was easy to see the strong relationship between Emily and her friends, and he was glad she'd had them beside her for all these years after everything that had happened to her. She hadn't talked about it since that day she first met Jane, but he knew that she'd been through hell, even after the adoption.

As the night wore on, he became more and more aware of Emily. Every time one of them moved, there would be some connection between them, arms brushing or legs pressing together. He'd had a semi all through dinner, and it was tortuous.

A few times their gazes connected, and they'd sit there staring at each other like fools, time standing still until someone interrupted and pulled their attention away. He caught a few meaningful looks pass between Emily and her friends and knew that they'd picked up on their mutual attraction the same as Jane had.

They'd just finished sharing a couple of plates of tiramisu when Emily's friend Amber directed her attention towards him, giving him an appraising look. She was an interesting woman; she seemed kind of arty and free-spirited, but then she'd get serious, and her spine of steel would make an appearance.

"You've been pretty quiet Brian," she observed. "I have to say I'm impressed you didn't feel compelled to dominate the conversation like a lot of men would in this situation."

He smiled. "It's fun seeing you ladies all get to know each other. Thanks for inviting me."

Emily shifted in her seat, making her thigh press more tightly against his. He heard her breath catch, but she didn't move away. Not that she had far to go, with the wall on her other side.

He slid his hand onto her thigh, just resting it on the denim, increasing their connection. To his surprise, she didn't push his hand away, and he felt her pushing her thighs together, showing him that she was just as affected as he was by their nearness.

The check came and after a brief scuffle, they decided to split it five ways. "That's how we usually do it when we go out together, we always just do an even split," Jenny told him and Jane. "It all balances out in the end, so don't mess up our system."

The five of them all threw their credit cards on the table and waited as the waiter rushed off to process their payments.

"I'm so glad you invited us," Jane said to Emily and her friends. "You guys are so much fun."

"You'll have to come out with again some time," Amber told her as the waiter brought back their receipts and she signed hers with a flourish. "OK kids, this has been great but I'm going to head out. I'm meeting my friend Andy for...um...drinks."

She slid out of the booth and gave them all a friendly wave. "See you girls later. And you too Brian."

Jenny rolled her eyes. "Drinks means benefits," she said drily as Amber hurried off.

Seeing their curious looks she added, "Those two were good friends in high school. It was platonic back then even though it was obvious to everyone except her that he was desperately in love with her. They reconnected at our twenty-fifth high school reunion a few months ago and he's been clear that he's into her and wants more, but she's only willing to be friends with benefits right now. Who knows why? They're together all the time."

Something tickled at Brian's brain but then Jenny's eyes widened in alarm, and he lost the thought. She glanced between Brian and Emily. "Oh sorry, should I not talk about this in front of Jane?"

Jane laughed. "I'm twenty-one Jenny. I know what friends with benefits is. I've even had one or two of my own."

Brian groaned. "Please, I don't need to hear this, I'm begging you."

Jane laughed, then looked down and started tapping on her phone. "Well on that note, I have an Uber coming, so I'm heading out too."

She leaned over and kissed Brian on the cheek. "Thanks for the game Uncle Brian, it was fun. I'll text you later. You too Emily."

Jane slid out of the booth and Jenny also moved to standing. "I'll go with you Jane, I need to get home too. Dave is probably wondering where I am by now."

She shot a meaningful look at Brian, then winked at her friend. "It was nice to meet you Brian. Can you make sure Emily gets home OK?"

"I can get home just fine," Emily protested, but Jenny was already rushing off after Jane, leaving the two of them alone.

Emily groaned. "Now everyone's in on the matchmaking, I guess."

Brian turned in his seat to look at Emily as the earlier explanation about Amber and Andy finally registered. "Wait! I think I know where we've met before!"

Emily

"Wait. We've met before? Is that why you seem so familiar?"

Brian looked at her excitedly. "It's been bugging me since we met that day in your office," he explained. "You seemed so familiar, but I assumed it was just because you and Jane look so much alike."

Emily gave him a curious look. She'd also felt this odd sense that they'd met somewhere.

"Did you go to a high school reunion at the Drake a few months ago?"

She nodded. "Yeah, that's where my twenty-fifth high school reunion was, how did you know that?"

"Did you happen to dance with a handsome stranger before you got pulled away by your friend who was having some sort of crisis?"

Emily's mouth dropped. "Oh my god! You're the guy I danced with that night? I'd totally forgotten about that with all the drama with Amber and Jenny that night. That was really you? Holy crap, that's such a strange coincidence."

She had a flash of a good looking blonde man crossing the room and pulling her close so they could dance to a Seal song. The light had been too dim to see him very well, but she remembered feeling surprisingly comfortable in his arms. She would have definitely pursued the obvious attraction between them if she hadn't had to leave.

She frowned as she realized that he must have come there with someone else. "You didn't go to my high school."

Brian shook his head. "No, I was there with my friend Lainie."

"Lainie Halverson? Oh yeah, I remember her, we didn't hang out together, but we had a lot of classes together." She paused. Oh my god, had she kissed someone's boyfriend?

"I didn't know you two were dating."

"Oh no, it's not like that," he reassured her. "We're just good friends. She's not in touch with anyone from high school anymore, and she felt weird about showing up at the reunion alone."

Emily nodded. "Yeah, I probably would too."

A heavy silence fell between them as she picked at the last bites of the tiramisu. This was such a weird situation, all the connections between them. There were so many ties, so many coincidences, it almost felt like they were fated to meet. But Emily didn't believe in fate.

"Well, I should probably head home now," she told him reluctantly. "They probably want this table."

He took her hand in his and she shivered. The look he gave her was both vulnerable and hopeful.

"How about coming back to my place for a night cap?"

Her eyes widened. "I don't think that's a good idea, Brian."

She really hoped he didn't ask why, because right now she was having a hard time coming up with an excuse. He tilted his head and met her gaze as he stroked her hand with one long finger. It made little zings move through her body, straight to her core.

"It seems like fate keeps throwing us in each other's path. The reunion. Jane. The Cubs game. It's got to mean something."

Clearly she wasn't the only one who thought that.

"I'm not looking for a relationship right now," she warned.

The truth was, she was never looking for a relationship, but she didn't share that. She'd had a couple of long-term boyfriends in high school and college, but since Jane was born she'd never dated the same person for more than two or three months. It felt too risky to get close or come to depend on someone else, so the minute they started to get serious or clingy she gave them the boot.

"How about we just spend some time together and see how thing go?" he suggested. "We don't need to plan out our entire future tonight. We can just have a drink, maybe make out a little. We both seemed to like that." He gave her a soft smile and she felt herself wavering.

"I don't want this to be weird for Jane."

"This has nothing to do with Jane, but given that she's practically throwing us together, I don't think we need to worry about her being upset about it."

She nodded, unable to think of any other reason to avoid doing what she wanted to do anyway. After all, they were both adults, both single, both old enough to understand the rules. Maybe if they spent more time together this crazy attraction between them would lessen.

"One drink," she finally said. "But that's it. Just a drink."

"One drink." He nodded. "I can totally do that."

Ten minutes later they were in an Uber. Their butts had scarcely hit the backseat before they leapt at each other, mouths meeting in a frantic crash of lips and teeth as they made out like they were teenagers. Brian knocked her ball cap off her head and threaded his fingers through her blonde hair, pulling on the strands while his tongue plundered her mouth. God, his kisses were like a drug, and all she could think about what getting more. Her entire body was on fire.

Emily pulled his Cubs jersey out of the waistband of his jeans and ran her fingers up and down his chest, lightly scratching her nails against his skin. She could feel her hardened nipples poking painfully against her bra. When they broke apart to catch their breath, her eyes caught on the impressive ridge of his hard-on, and she licked her lips.

Brian growled, then lowered his head to nip his teeth down her neck before returning to her mouth for another passionate kiss. Her leg moved across his, trying to get closer to him.

They heard the sound of someone clearing their throat, followed by an irritated voice saying, "Hey! How about you guys knock it off? We're here already."

They broke apart sheepishly. They'd been so distracted by their make-out session they'd both forgotten that they had an audience.

Emily imagined that the Uber driver saw a lot of risqué things in this backseat, but her cheeks heated nonetheless. They were grown ass adults in their forties, not some horny college kids.

Brian grabbed her hand and practically dragged her up the stairs to his place. She thrilled at the fact that she'd affected him as much as he affected her. It wasn't like Emily to be out of control like this, but then again she'd never been this attracted to anyone before. Ever.

Brian opened his door, throwing his keys in the direction of a nearby table. They hit the floor with a crash as he rounded on her, pressing her back against the front door as his lips descended on hers again.

"Emily. God."

She had the impression that he'd lost his power of speech. She understood the feeling.

He grabbed her thighs and boosted her against the door, his hard cock nestling in heated cradle of her legs as he kissed her again. She rolled her hips against him, desperate for more friction.

The next time they broke apart Brian ripped her jersey up over her head and relieved her of her bra faster than she could process. She returned the favor, drawing his shirt over his head before leaning down to run her tongue up the side of his neck.

His groaned loudly. "Emily. If you want to stop, you need to tell me now."

She lifted her head and met his eyes, the decision simple. "Don't stop."

"Be sure Emily. I want nothing more than to be inside you, but we can wait."

She nodded decisively. "I'm sure."

His eyes widened in excitement, and he turned with her legs still wrapped around his waist. She laughed and tapped his shoulder, making him stop so she could slide down to her own feet.

"Let's not go crazy there, old man. I can walk."

He grabbed her hand and practically ran to the bedroom at the end of the hall, dragging her behind him. Slamming the bedroom door open with a bang, Brian placed one hand on her chest and gently pushed her backwards until the back of her knees hit the bed. She plopped down with a laugh and watched as he removed his pants and boxers with one big push.

Brian stood in front of her, gloriously naked, his engorged cock practically winking at her. The lights were off in the bedroom, but between the reflection of the streetlights through the windows and the light from the hallway, the room was bathed in a soft light, giving her the perfect view of exactly how much he wanted her. Emily slid off the bed and moved onto her knees in front of him.

"What are you doing?" His question sounded choked.

"I just want a taste," she promised, looking up at him from beneath her eyelashes. She licked her lips.

He groaned as she leaned forward and circled her tongue around the mushroom head of his cock, swirling around and around before finally taking him deeper. She moved up and down quickly, pushing forward until the tip of his cock hit her throat, then sliding off again. Brian's entire body was taut, and she knew that he was struggling to hold himself in check. Emily loved the rush of power she felt giving head, especially with this man. She ran her tongue along the underside of his cock before releasing him with a pop.

"You taste good."

"My turn," he growled, his voice so deep that Emily felt a rush of moisture flood her already soaked panties. He was usually so easy-going. She had no idea he had this bossy side, but she had to say she really liked it.

He pulled her up to standing, grabbed her by the waist, and tossed her on the bed. She landed with a bounce, laughing as he got to work dragging her jeans and sodden panties down her legs. He threw them over his shoulder, then pulled her butt to the edge of the mattress.

Brian kneeled next to the bed, drawing her legs over his shoulders as he went in for a taste. The first touch of his rough tongue on the tender flesh of her center almost made her levitate off the bed. He explored her slick folds with his tongue, alternating between slow licks and sharp taps against her clit until she was squirming and moaning incoherently.

She was close, so close, and based on the satisfied look on his face, he well knew it. She almost cried as he moved away from her. "Let me get a condom."

Emily scooted up higher on the bed, watching him frantically search through a drawer in the bedside table. He tossed several items on the floor before raising his hand triumphantly, a square package between his long fingers.

"Found one!" he said triumphantly. "It's been a while since I've needed one of these."

She watched while he made quick of the protection, appreciating that he didn't make it a big deal like some guys did. She had an IUD, so birth control was covered, but they hadn't discussed their health yet.

Brian crawled over her body, notching his latex-covered cock in the cradle of her thighs as he settled his forearms on either side of her, holding part of his weight off her.

"Are you ready for me?" he asked as he stared down at her, eyes burning with desire.

She nodded.

"I need your words, Emily," he told her.

She felt a rush of gratitude. Knowing her history, she appreciated him being absolutely sure that he had her consent. It had taken a long time after the attack before she felt comfortable having sex again, and even longer before the nightmares stopped.

"Do it Brian," she told him, her voice strong and sure. "Fuck me. Now."

He slid in slowly, taking his time and allowing her to accommodate to his girth. It had been a while for her, so she appreciated his courtesy. Her muscles were burning as they stretched around him, and she took a deep breath to help them release.

"Oh my god, you feel so good, so tight," he whispered as he bottomed out inside her.

She felt deliciously full. Emily bent her knees and opened them out to the side, rolling her pelvis higher towards him. "Move!" she ordered.

He chuckled but complied with her request, sliding almost all the way out before punching back down quickly. He repeated the action a few times and she moaned at the incredible sensation of their bodies connecting. Brian's skin was rough against the softness of her own body, his lightly furred chest scraping across her chest and teasing her already sensitive nipples.

Brian leaned down and kissed her deeply and she wrapped her legs around his hips, tilting her pelvis and drawing him closer as he began to pick up speed.

"Oh my god, I'm close already," she gasped.

Brian redoubled his efforts, pounding into her so quickly that all she could do was hold on. She loved that he didn't treat her like she was fragile, especially with her history. Every hard thrust drew his pelvis over hers, further stimulating her already engorged clit. Suddenly her entire body tightened, her toes curling as her orgasm rushed through her body.

"Brian!"

She wailed his name as her muscles spasmed against him, squeezing him until he succumbed to his own pleasure. He came with a long shout, and Emily felt the warmth of his release inside her, even through the barrier of the condom. He jerked a few more times then collapsed on top of her, burying his face in the crook of her neck.

They lay there a long time until their sweat cooled, and their heart rates slowed. Brian finally rolled off her to take care of the condom. He wrapped it in a Kleenex, and she felt the loss of their connection until he returned to her side. He pulled the blanket up and shifted to cuddle her against his side. She nestled against him, her head on his shoulder.

"Wow." Emily really couldn't think of another word that better described the situation.

"Yeah, I agree."

Brian kissed the top of her head, one hand rubbing her back tenderly. "That was way better than I imagined, and for the record, I've imagined it several times and it was always fabulous."

She laughed, thinking that he'd probably ruined for other men with that performance.

"Well, that's one way for me to break a dry spell." At his curious look she explained, "It's been over a year for me."

He nodded, then looked thoughtful. "About the same for me too, maybe even eighteen months," he admitted. "I usually last a little longer, for the record."

"Well in that case," she drawled, "We should really try that again. Practice makes perfect."

Brian

"Can you tell me more about Jane when she was little?"

They had just finished their second round of lovemaking, and had collapsed into an exhausted heap, limbs tangled around each other. Emily turned her head and looked up at Brian from where she rested on his chest, her gaze soft and vulnerable. The urge to comfort her was strong, and he rubbed his hand over her back soothingly.

"My sister had leukemia when she was a kid," he started. Emily inhaled in surprise.

"I don't think Jane even knows about that. She recovered and was fine, thank god, but the treatments left her infertile. She convinced herself that no one would ever want to marry her since she was, as she called it, 'barren'. But then she met my brother-in-law, and he broke through all of her barriers and they fell deeply in love. He told her that he didn't care if she could birth a child, that if they wanted kids the world was full of tiny humans looking for a home."

"He sounds like a great guy."

"Yeah, he was," Brian said fondly. "The best husband I could have imagined for my sister. They had a long engagement, partly because I'm pretty sure my sister thought he would change his mind about her, and as soon as they got married they started the process to get approved for adoption. It took a really long time, what with all the checks they do, and I guess there's not as many kids available for adoption in this country like there used to be years ago."

Emily lowered her head to his chest and wrapped her arm around his waist as he continued. He tightened his arm around her, loving the feeling of her pressed against him.

"They were over the moon when they found out that they'd been matched with a baby. I've never seen two people so excited to be parents like those two. It wasn't as common back then, but my brother-in-law insisted that he take a paternity leave at the same time my sister was off work for maternity leave, so that they could both bond with Jane."

"They kept her name, Jane. That's the name I gave her in the hospital."

Brian nodded. "They had picked out a few other names, but when they saw her they knew she was a Jane. My sister said it felt right, like it was a way to honor your sacrifice."

Emily nodded. "I really appreciate that. What was Jane like as a baby?" Emily asked.

"She was always super vocal. Not colicky really, just always making noise, cooing, screeching, giggling, and then when she was old enough, she started chattering and singing. She was a cute little thing with her blonde hair and big blue eyes, just like yours. People used to say she looked like one of the Precious Moments figurines, you know the ones people used to collect?"

Emily chuckled. "Yeah, Jenny loved those damn things when we were kids."

"Jane had this stuffed elephant that she used to drag around everywhere. She got it from Santa Claus when she was two, and I don't think she stopped carrying it until she went to kindergarten. She called him 'Mr. Ella' because she couldn't say 'elephant'. It was freaking adorable. And you know, she still has that ratty old thing on a shelf in her bedroom."

He felt Emily's lips curl into a smile against the skin of his chest.

"She was super social and had a pretty diverse circle of friends. When she lived here she was constantly texting or talking to someone. Everyone is a friend to our girl."

"What else?"

"She always loved sports. She went out for cross-country, volleyball, and softball, and of course you know she's a diehard fan of the Cubbies. But she also did pretty well in school, mostly As and Bs, and even after her parents died she never let her studies suffer."

"Jane said they died in a car crash?" she asked. "I didn't want to ask her for details in case it was too painful to talk about."

He nodded. "Yeah, Jane was a freshman in high school, and she called me at work one day because her parents didn't come to pick her up from volleyball like they'd promised, and they weren't answering their cell phones. I went to pick her up and when we got back to their house, there were state troopers pulling into the driveway. Their car hit a patch of ice on the Dan Ryan – you know how everyone is always driving so fast when the traffic is actually moving on the expressway – and they crashed head-on into one of concrete dividers going at a high speed. The only blessing was that it looked they died instantly."

"Jesus Christ, that's terrible."

"Yeah, we were devastated, of course. We were both walking around in a fog for months. I considered moving into my sister's house so Jane could stay in the environment she'd always known, but her parents were upside down on their mortgage and we needed to take a loss and get out from under it."

She made a sympathetic noise and he continued, "I moved Jane in here with me and tried to keep things as normal as possible for her. I was worried that she'd be upset about changing schools, but it turned out that she liked her school here in the city better. It was an adjustment for both of us, and it was challenging to figure out how to parent a teenage girl who was grieving. But she and I had always been close, especially since I didn't have kids of my own, so it made the transition much easier, all things considered."

"I hope she's not too disappointed now that she knows the story about her birth parents," Emily said softly. "I had the impression she thought her parents would be star crossed lovers or something."

Emily's voice was small and sad, and Brian wondered if she thought she was somehow lacking. He tightened his arm around her and gave her a firm squeeze.

"She was thrilled to finally meet you Emily, and she's been so excited to get to know you. Jane's heart is enormous, and I know she already loves you. You should also know that she would have searched for you even if her parents hadn't died. She told me that they'd all agreed that she would try to meet her birth parents when she was old enough."

"In that case I'm glad I agreed to have the records unsealed when she was twenty-one," Emily told him. "I debated about it during the entire pregnancy. The whole experience was so horrible, and I worried incessantly about if I was making the right decision. Jenny and Amber encouraged me, they said that when the time came I could always refuse contact, but if I requested that they were permanently sealed I'd never have the chance to even consider meeting her again."

"I'm glad you did."

"I felt so traumatized at the time that I couldn't imagine ever meeting my daughter and having it be OK. But it is OK, and I'm glad she found me. I really am. She's better than I could have ever imagined. I always mourned her absence in my life, you know, but now that I've spent time with her, I couldn't imagine not having her around."

They lapsed into silence for a few minutes, each lost in their own thoughts.

"Can I ask you a personal question?" he finally asked.

"Well, I'm sprawled over your chest buck naked," she pointed out with a smile in her voice. "I guess that entitles you to at least one personal question."

"Did you ever think about having another child?"

She stiffened for a moment, then took a deep breath and relaxed again. "No, I...I couldn't go through that again. I knew I would feel guilty about keeping one child after I gave away another. I decided after Jane was born that I would never have another child and I've never regretted that decision."

She raised her head and studied his face, as if looking for signs of judgement, and he leaned forward and kissed her on the tip of the nose. She gave him a small smile, then crinkled her brow.

"What about you?" She stiffened. "Oh my god, I never even asked you if you were single. Is there a girlfriend somewhere who's going to come in here and stab me or something?"

"Naw," he scoffed. "No girlfriend. For the record I wouldn't do that. But the truth is that I haven't dated a lot since my sister died. I needed to focus on Jane. She became my top priority, and that didn't leave time for anything serious in my personal life. At least until now."

He met her eyes and decided to put himself out there. "I know you said you weren't looking for anything serious Emily, but the truth is, I like you a lot and I could see us getting serious. This thing between us is like nothing I've ever experienced, and I know you feel it too."

"Brian..."

He gave her another squeeze. "Hear me out. Can we just agree to keep seeing each other and see where this goes? We don't need to make a commitment right now, but can we commit to seeing if we want to commit?"

"What does that even mean?" she laughed.

"We date exclusively and see how it goes."

"I don't know...," she prevaricated.

"Woman, I just gave you two incredibly good orgasms and if you give me a little recovery time I know I could make it a solid three. Can you take a leap with me? Please?"

There was a long pause, and he could practically hear her brain working.

"Well, it's hard to say no to incredibly good orgasms, so how about this? We'll try this thing, and if it it's not working for either of us, we cut it off immediately, no hard feelings. We're bound to see each other with Jane in common, and it's important that if things don't work out it won't impact her in any way."

"Agreed."

"Let's keep this just between us for a while."

"Why?" he asked. "Are you ashamed of me or something?"

She laughed. "Of course not, doofus. I just, well I want this to be private until we figure out what we're doing. If everyone around us knows, if Jane knows, it'll create expectations. I don't want to do that, not until we know if this thing is going to last."

"OK," he answered reluctantly. "I won't talk about it, but if she asks me directly I'm not going to lie about it either."

"Understood. Do we need to shake on it or something?" she asked.

"I think I've had enough recovery time now," he told her. "Let's see if I can get your legs shaking instead."

Emily

A month later...

"Hey girls, sorry I'm late. I had a conference call that ran long."

Emily rushed across the lobby of the theater and gave Jenny and Amber each a hug. "Should we grab a drink and find our seats?"

The three friends had a longstanding agreement that at least once every month they would get together in real life and do something together. They'd stuck to their agreement pretty consistently in the twenty-one years since they graduated college and stopped being roommates. It helped that they all lived in the Chicagoland area. But it also reflected their commitment to be there for each other, regardless of boyfriends or jobs or whatever else was going on in their lives.

Tonight they were seeing some theater performance that Amber had picked out. She'd been a theater geek in high school and worked as a fundraiser for a local arts organization, so Amber was always in the know on Chicago's hottest new shows.

The stopped at the concession stand and purchased glasses of wine, then headed into the auditorium. Like many of the city's small theaters, this space had been given a second life after the church that used to in the building had left the area. The auditorium was ringed with beautiful stained glass windows, and the seats were all converted church pews. Finding their aisle, the three friends slid into the middle of one of the long benches and settled in.

"How's everyone today?" Amber asked, giving them both a smile over the top of her glass. "You start Jenny." Amber was the bossiest of the group.

"Things are going great," Jenny started. "Work is good. Dave is good. I have no complaints."

Dave and Jenny had been friends in high school, until the night he took her virginity and then humiliated her. She'd spent the next twenty-five years hating him but then they'd reunited at their twenty-fifth reunion, the same even where Emily had met Brian. Dave and Jenny had a rocky start, but they had worked things out and were not a nauseatingly sweet couple.

"Is you still talking about moving in together?" Emily asked.

Jenny nodded. "Yeah, it makes sense, we sleep over at each other's place most nights anyway. I can never find anything because half my stuff is at his place and the rest is at home. We just need to figure out where we are going to live. We both love our places, so we're both being a bit stubborn about it because neither of us wants to move."

"You could both sell and buy a new place," Emily suggested.

"Yeah, I'm pretty sure that's what we'll wind up doing," Jenny said. "It's all a negotiation. But enough about me. How's it going with Jane? And how's Brian?"

Emily felt a flush rise up her pale skin. "Well, Jane is great, but she knows Brian and I are dating now."

Her two friends looked at her expectantly and she continued her story. "As you know, we agreed we would keep it on the down-low for a little while so it wouldn't be awkward for her if it didn't work out. Unfortunately, something more awkward happened."

Emily paused to take a drink of her merlot and Amber asked, "Did she walk in on you two doing the nasty?"

She rolled her eyes. "God, no, not quite that awkward. But this morning she dropped by Brian's house unexpectedly and found me standing in the kitchen making coffee."

"So?"

"I was wearing Brian's shirt, and nothing else, with my hair dripping wet because we'd just gotten out of the shower. If that wasn't enough of a clue what was going on, he walked into the kitchen right after her, wearing just his boxers, his hair also wet. I'm sure we both looked like two kids who just caught by their parents."

Her two friends laughed. "Then what happened?" Amber asked.

"Well, first Brian and I got dressed. Then we had a conversation with her about not popping in unannounced anymore. It was all good though. Jane was ecstatic, you know she's been wanting to get us together for a while now."

"How do you feel about it all?" Jenny asked. "That's a big step for you two."

"Honestly it's kind of a relief. Even though it was my idea to hold off on telling Jane, I felt super awkward every time we talked or got together, especially when she was giving me all these not-so-subtle hints about getting together with Brian. So at least it's all out in the open now."

Emily shot a look at Amber, desperate to change the subject. "Speaking about open secrets, how's Andy?"

The lights dimmed and Amber laughed. "Oh damn, we're out of time. Thanks for playing."

Emily and Jenny exchanged looks in the dim light. Eventually this Amber and Andy relationship was going to come to a head. They'd been in a holding pattern of friends with benefits ever since the reunion earlier this summer. Eventually Andy would get tired of waiting for her, and they would either need to become a real couple or stop seeing each other. Either way, the fall-out would likely be difficult.

The next morning Emily woke up and took the El over to Jane's house. She and her daughter had been taking a Saturday morning Zumba class together as a bonding activity. She really liked hanging out with Jane. She didn't have that air of snotty entitlement that kids in their twenties often had. Plus, Zumba was a blast. Neither of them was particularly coordinated, but they had a great time getting their workout in, and they usually went for coffee afterwards.

She and Jane had easily fallen into a weekly routine, and Emily loved it. Her daughter seemed to enjoy spending time together as much as Emily did. They had lots in common and despite their long separation, it almost felt like they had been in each other's lives the entire time.

Jane shared an apartment with three other girls on the near north side. The building was a bit run down, but in a good neighborhood and close to the train. The girls all worked in professional jobs downtown and seemed to have good heads on their shoulders. Jane had told her that none of them were that into parties or nightlife.

One of Jane's roommates let her in, telling Emily that Jane was in the kitchen. Her daughter sat at the kitchen island, staring at some papers, and chewing her bottom lip nervously.

"Good morning," Emily said. "Is everything OK?"

Jane looked up, her expression clearing. "Oh hey Emily, yeah everything is fine. I just got a letter telling me that my deferment period was over and it's time to start paying my student loans. I'm having a bit of sticker shock about how much I owe."

It wasn't really her business, but Emily couldn't help but ask, "How bad is it?"

"Just under fifty thousand in total, plus interest will start accruing now."

Emily gasped. "Holy crap. Fifth thousand dollars? Didn't you have any scholarships?"

"I didn't get any scholarships other than a really small one that was like two thousand dollars a year. That barely covered my books. The thing was, my grades were good, and I was involved in athletics and extracurriculars, but I wasn't the best of the best at any of those things. I couldn't compete with all the other kids going to Northwestern."

"What about financial aid?"

"I received some, but I didn't qualify for a lot of aid because of Brian's income," Jane explained. "It's not like he's loaded, but we were in this weird spot where we were too poor to afford Northwestern on our own but too rich to qualify for most financial aid. I had some money in a college savings account from my parents' life insurance, so I was able to use that to help pay some of my tuition, and of course I lived at Uncle Brian's house, so I didn't have to pay rent anywhere, but even still I had to take out a lot of loans. My uncle offered to take out a second mortgage on his apartment, but I didn't feel right asking him to do that."

"Oh my god, I'm so sorry. That's terrible."

One good thing about Emily's parents was that they had paid for all four years of her tuition. Her father was a doctor, and her mother was an attorney, so they could afford it. She'd had to work part-time and in the summers to pay for books and other expenses like food and entertainment, but otherwise everything else was covered. When they disowned her, they'd already paid for her last year of college, so she was able to graduate debt-free as planned even after they cut her off.

"Well, that's what it's like to be a college graduate in this country I guess," Jane said. "Hopefully it will pay off in the long run. I'll just need to cut down on expenses for a while. Anyway, it's time for class. Let me just go get my shoes and we can go."

After Jane left Emily looked around furtively to make sure she was alone, then pulled out her phone. Glancing down at the papers that her daughter had left on the counter, she took pictures and saved them to her phone. She knew she was violating Jane's privacy, but she made a good salary and had some money in savings. Maybe she could find a way to help her daughter.

"You ready?" Jane asked when she returned a minute later.

"Yep." Emily slid the phone back into her pocket. She would worry about Jane's loans later.

The dance studio was a few blocks away and as they walked, Jane brought up the subject of Brian. Her daughter must have been really distracted by her student loan situation because she already knew Jane well enough to know that she wasn't one to wait when she was curious about something.

"Sorry again about walking in on you and Brian," she started.

"It's no problem," Emily responded. "You had no way of knowing. I'm just sorry you had to find out that way."

Thankfully, Jane hadn't seen too much. If she had come over twenty minutes earlier she would have walked in on her uncle railing Emily against the shower wall. They might be in their forties, but Emily and Brian had the libidos of a much younger couple. They couldn't get enough of each other and spent almost every night at each other's place. It felt like things were getting serious between the two of them, and she tried not to think about that too much so she wouldn't panic.

"So...things are going well with you two, huh?" Jane asked slyly.

"They're going pretty well," Emily responded, her tone guarded. She was naturally private, but it felt really weird to discuss Brian with Emily. Their situation was really messy and talking to her daughter about dating her uncle didn't seem appropriate.

"You two make a great couple," Jane told her. "I really hope it works out for you. Who knows, maybe someday you'll be my mom AND my aunt."

Emily stopped and turned to face her daughter. "Your uncle and I promised each other we would try not to make things uncomfortable for you if...I mean when, we break up. I just want to be clear that my relationship with Brian is completely separate from my relationship with you. Nothing that happens with him will affect how I feel about you."

Jane linked her arm in hers and they resumed walking. "I get that Emily, and I appreciate it, believe me. But Uncle Brian put his life on hold for me for a long time, and after all that you went through, well, I just want what's best for both of you. I just hope that turns out to be the two of you together. If not, we'll all deal. Either way we're going to be one big happy family. Now let's go get our Zumba on."

Brian

Brian looked across the dining room table and gave Emily a smile. They had both been swamped at work this week and instead of putting in extra hours in the office tonight, they'd agreed to bring some work home and do it together. They shared a thin crust pizza – the real Chicago pizza to everyone except the tourists – while tapping away on their laptops.

After a couple of hours of focused work, Emily closed her laptop and pushed her chair away from the table.

"You done?"

She nodded. "How about you?"

Brian saved his file, closed his laptop, and took off his reading glasses. "I can be."

"Oh good," Emily said as she stalked around the table with a sultry smile. "Because working across from you has been torture."

"Oh yeah?"

"Yeah." She slid between him and the table, got on his lap, and straddled his hips. "You're way too distracting."

"What did I do?" he asked.

"You were just sitting there looking so handsome, it was terrible. I know you wear those reading glasses just to torture me with your hot professor vibe."

He laughed. He loved this playful side of Emily. After six weeks of dating, she had become more and more open and comfortable with him. They hadn't talked about the future, taking things day by day, but it definitely felt like they were heading in that direction.

He reached up and palmed her breasts, one in each hand. He could feel her nipples harden against his palms.

"Hot professor, huh? Maybe you're gonna have to punish me for distracting you."

Her eyes darkened. "Maybe I will."

She looked thoughtful for a moment, then slid off his lap. "Here's what you're going to do. You're going to pull your chair away from the table to face me and put your hands behind you. Hold onto the back of the chair and don't let go until I tell you to."

He was instantly hard. "What happens if I let go?"

"I stop."

Brian pushed his chair out and dutifully reached around to grip the back of the chair.

"Remember," she warned. "Don't let go."

Emily kneeled in front of him and met his gaze. Giving him a saucy wink, she began to slowly unbutton the buttons of his shirt. She pulled it off his shoulders, and he moved to free his arms so she could fully remove it.

She gave his chest a sharp slap and pushed him back against the chair, so the back of his shirt was trapped by his body weight.

"Ah ah ah Mister, I said not to move!" she reminded him in a stern voice.

His sleeves were wrapped around his biceps, restraining him a bit, and it heightened his excitement. Emily leaned forward and gave him a quick hard kiss on the lips, before sliding her lips down to his neck. She licked along the column of his throat, scattering tiny kisses along the way, and then nipped his collar bone. He groaned.

"Be good," she reminded him.

She licked around his nipple, laving it with her tongue before biting it between her teeth. He inhaled sharply at the sting of pain. She gave the other nipple the same treatment before sliding her tongue down his abdomen. Having her on her knees, moving so slowly, being unable to touch her, it was torture.

She looked up at him beneath her lashes, then unbuckled his belt and opened his zipper, pulling the fabric apart. The room was silent other than the sound of his increasingly fast breathing. Emily grabbed his waistband and slid his boxers down just under his balls. His painfully hard cock popped up and hit his stomach, dripping with pre-cum. She laughed.

Leaning forward, Emily took his cock in one hand, and lightly gripped his balls in her other. He groaned again. "Emily!"

Ignoring him, she wrapped her mouth around his length, sliding up and down, circling the roughness of her tongue against his sensitive tip. Back and forth she went, following her mouth with her hand, applying suction until he was beside himself with desire.

He reached to touch her hair and she immediately pulled off. "What did I tell you?" she asked, her voice firm.

He reached back to grasp the chair again, but couldn't resist telling her, "Two can play this game, you know."

She gave him a grin. "Oh good. Did I have a recurring fantasy where you tie me to your bed and lick every inch of my body before fucking my brains out while I'm immobilized beneath you?"

He groaned at that visual, his mind racing with ideas how to play out that little fantasy.

Emily took him in her mouth again and squeezed his balls. His orgasm barreled down his spine with the force of a runaway freight train.

"I'm coming," he bit out a second before he shot his seed into her mouth in long spurts. Emily sucked him down until he collapsed against the chair with a loud groan.

"Fuck."

She sat back on her heels and giggled, wiping her mouth with her hand. "That was sure fun."

"God, I love you so much."

His head snapped up as he realized what he said. He hadn't meant to tell her. Not yet. But it was true. He was hopelessly in love with her.

Emily looked shocked and a tiny bit panicked. He was suddenly terrified that she would run away. Releasing his hold on the chair, he pulled her up on her knees again and slid his hands down her arms until he could link his fingers with hers. He squeezed her fingers between his and watched her until she met his gaze.

"I know it's early and you don't need to say anything back, but I just wanted you to know how I feel. Please don't freak out."

"Brian." Her eyes looked troubled.

He leaned forward a bit more until his lips were almost touching hers. "For now, it's enough that you know how I feel. I can wait for you to get there. I'm a very patient man."

"I..um..."

He shook his head, and moved to standing, pulling her with him. "How about we talk about this more later? For right now, I'd love to try out another fantasy."

Emily

The next day she had just walked into her house when the mail carrier knocked on the door. "Certified mail for Ms. Emily Langdon?"

"Yes that's me," she said, signing the tablet and taking the envelope.

She stared at it for a long time, feeling unaccountably nervous to open it. The return address was from a law firm in the city, but not one she recognized. Why on Earth would she be getting certified mail from a law firm at her house? Was someone suing her for something?

She opened the letter with shaking fingers.

Dear Ms. Langdon,

This letter is to notify you that our firm has been retained to represent the estate of Mr. and Mrs. Edward Langdon. The decedents named you as the sole heir to their estate. Please contact our office at your earliest convenience to schedule a reading of the will and to begin the process of transferring your inherited assets. You can reach me at 312-555-5555 extension 24. Please accept our deepest sympathies for your loss.

Sincerely,

John Archer, Esq.

Emily read the letter again, then slid down the wall to sit on the floor. She realized with a start that this was the second time in the space of a couple of months that she'd received a letter so shocking that her legs gave out.

Deceased? Sole heir? What did this mean?

She read the letter two more times, but it still didn't make any sense. She reached into her bag, looking for her phone. It was after six, but she figured that she would leave a message for the attorney so they could talk tomorrow. To her surprise, he picked up on the second ring.

"John Archer."

"Oh, hi, I didn't expect you to answer. My name is Emily Langdon, and I just got a letter from you about my parents, Edward and Elena Langdon."

"Oh yes, Ms. Langdon, I'm very sorry for your loss."

"Thank you, but I didn't realize that my parents were, um, that they had passed away. Can you tell me what happened?"

The attorney cleared his throat, as if he was uncomfortable being in the position to give her bad news.

"It was a gas leak. The investigators think that some construction work in the yard dislodged a gas line, filling the house with gas while they slept. The workers noticed that the house was filled with gas the next morning and the immediately called the Fire Department. Upon searching the house, they found your parents dead in their bed. If it's any consolation, they appear to have passed away peacefully. I'm so sorry you had to hear about it like this."

"It's fine," she responded. "We were estranged, and it's been over twenty years since we were in contact with each other. I think you must have made a mistake, there's no way my parents left me anything in their will."

"Your parents were clients of mine for many years Ms. Langdon. There's been no mistake here, but it's probably better for us to talk about this in person. Can you come to my office tomorrow? We can review the will and then I'll try to answer any questions you may have."

"Sure, would four o'clock work?"

"Yes, that'll be fine Ms. Langdon. I'll see you then."

She hung up the phone and sat staring at the letter for a long time. Her parents were dead, and she didn't know how to feel about it. They had been terrible parents, and they had rejected her when she needed them the most. Any chance they had to step up and repair the relationship had died with them.

She took a deep breath and welcomed the familiar numbness. It was the shield that had served her well whenever something traumatic happened. She sat there staring into space for several minutes before unlocking her phone again and texting Brian.

"Can you come over? It's important."

She realized with a start that her first thought had been to text Brian, not Amber and Jenny. She didn't want to analyze that too much right now, not with all these confused thoughts swirling through her mind. She'd call them later. Her phone beeped with a response.

"I'll be there in thirty minutes."

Brian

As soon as he received Emily's text Brian jumped in the car and headed north to her house. Her message had been short and cryptic, but he could read through the lines that something big was happening, and he knew instinctively that it was something bad.

Was she breaking up with him? He didn't think that was it. Things had been going great between them. They had been together almost every day the last two months, and their relationship seemed solid. The transition into being a couple had felt shockingly easy.

They both had their own lives, but they also enjoyed spending time together, whether they were hanging out with Jane, going out somewhere, or just sitting in front of the fire reading in their pajamas. She'd even made him start running on the lakefront with her, insisting that he needed to work on his cardio to protect his heart. He hated running, but he did it to make her happy.

Unless she was still freaked out about his declaration of love last night? She'd seemed OK when she left this morning, but then again she'd also told him that she wanted to be alone tonight instead of hanging out with him. He'd tried not to read anything into that.

With all these thoughts swirling around in his head, Brian didn't know what to expect when he got there. Emily answered the door wearing her work clothes, her face scarily blank. He realized that the last time he'd seen that face on her was when she told Jane about being attacked. It was like a mask she put on when she was traumatized.

Pulling her into his arms, Brian pressed a kiss on top of her head. "What is it? What happened?"

She pulled away from him and headed to the kitchen. "I need a drink first."

He followed her, watching as she dug out a bottle of Jameson from the cabinet and poured them both a shot, leaving the bottle on the kitchen table between them. She collapsed onto a chair and downed her shot in one quick gulp. He watched her with concern.

"What's wrong Emily?" he asked. "You look like you've seen a ghost."

"My parents are dead."

He sat back. That was one of the last things he expected her to hear. "What? How did you find out?"

She pulled a crumpled up letter out of her suit jacket pocket and slid it across the table. He read it once, and then again, while she poured herself another shot and knocked it back in one gulp.

"Your parents named you as their heir?" he asked. "I thought you haven't talked to them since you got pregnant."

She nodded and eyed the Jameson bottle. He slid it farther away from her and she shot him a half-hearted glare.

"It's been almost twenty-two years since we last had contact," she confirmed. "I called the attorney, and he assured me that it wasn't a mistake. I'm their sole beneficiary, whatever that means. I'm going to see him tomorrow at four to review the will and do the paperwork."

"I'll go with you," he responded instantly.

When she opened her mouth to object he added sternly, "You shouldn't do this alone. If you don't want me to come, then bring Jenny or Amber."

She nodded. "No, you're right. I want you to come, thank you."

"Do you want to talk about it?"

She shook her head. "I need time to process this, and I want to hear what the attorney has to say. It's weird, you know, hearing about them after all this time. Other than when I told Jane what happened, I hadn't thought about them for years. I had no idea if they were dead or alive but now that I know that they're dead, I don't know how to feel."

"You don't need to feel anything," he reassured her, rubbing her arm. "I'm here for you Emily, and I'll support you no matter what. Just tell me what you need, baby."

She leaned forward and kissed him briefly.

"I need junk food and to watch something mindless on TV."

"You got it."

The spent the evening cuddled up on the couch eating chips and ice cream and watching reality TV. When Emily fell into an exhausted sleep, he carried her to bed and cuddled in behind her, keeping his arms around her until morning.

The next day he and Emily met outside the attorney's office a little before four o'clock. Emily was dressed conservatively, her hair pulled up in a bun, her expression carefully blank. He took her hand, and it was cold to the touch. He expected her to be nervous or unsettled, but she was completely emotionless. It worried him.

After checking in with the receptionist, they were led to a large conference room. Brian looked around, noting the high end furnishings. This was not a budget law firm, that's for sure. The place screamed old money. They waited less than five minutes before an older white man in a fancy suit strode into the conference room.

"Ms. Langdon? I'm John Archer, one of the partners here. We spoke on the phone."

Emily shook his hand. "Please call me Emily. This is my boyfriend Brian McKenna."

Archer shook his hand and after offering them drinks, invited them to be seated at the shiny wooden conference table. Brian helped Emily into her chair, then pulled his own as close to her as possible. He took her hand under the table.

"I need to formally read the will, and then I can answer any questions, does that sound OK Emily?"

"Sure."

"It's pretty short," Archer shared. He read through the typical legalese about being of sound mind before he got to the inheritance section.

"Upon the death of both parties, we hereby bequeath all our worldly possessions to our daughter Emily Jane Langdon, including our properties in Illinois and Florida, all funds deposited in investment accounts, and the balance remaining in our accounts at Chicago National Bank after payment of final expenses. We also leave a letter in the possession of our attorney, John Archer, to be passed onto Emily Jane Langdon following the reading of this last will and testament."

Archer finished reading the will and slid a sealed envelope across the table to Emily. "This is the letter that they wanted you to have."

"Thank you. I'll read it later," Emily said, slipping the envelope into her purse. She looked shell shocked, and Brian already knew her well enough to know that she was working hard to keep it together. He squeezed her hand.

"Very well," Archer said. "A few housekeeping items. Your parents requested no service. They asked to be cremated immediately upon death, and to have their ashes interned spread in Lake Michigan. I'll messenger the cremains to your house, if that works, so you can do the honors?"

Emily nodded, and Archer continued, "We'll be processing the paperwork to transfer the two properties to your ownership. I'll just need you to sign off on some paperwork for me. The property in Illinois was last valued at just over $700,000 and the property in Florida has a value of $967,000. Both are paid in full and current on taxes. It's up to you, of course, whether you want to keep the properties or sell them."

Emily nodded again. Brian was starting to worry about her, it wasn't like her to be so quiet.

"We've also run the value of the investments, life insurance, and cash on hand. After paying for their final expenses and the legal fees to settle the estate, you'll be left with just over two million dollars."

"What?" Emily gasped. "Two million dollars? I'm inheriting two million dollars? Are you serious?"

"Technically it's two million dollars plus a million and a half in property assets," Archer clarified.

When Emily continued to stare at him like he was crazy, Archer asked, "Didn't you know that your parents were wealthy?"

"Not a clue. I mean, they paid for my college, and we lived in a nice house, but I had no idea that they had that kind of money. How did that even happen?"

"Your parents both had very well-paying jobs, and by all reports they lived well below their means. Their vacation condo in Florida appears to be their only extravagance. They drove older cars, both of which are in the garage of their house by the way, and the lived a very simple life. Their frugal lifestyle coupled with their wise investment strategy means that you are now a wealthy woman Ms. Langdon. Congratulations."

Emily

What the actual fuck? Emily stared at the attorney with her mouth open, trying to process what she'd just heard. She made good money, enough to be firmly upper middle class, so it wasn't like she was hurting for money. But this? This was next level.

How was it possible that she'd inherited a small fortune from the people who had ruthlessly cut her out of their lives when she was attacked? They had never even tried to contact her in all these years and now she found out that they'd named her their sole heir? Her head was spinning.

"This has to be a mistake," she finally said. "I haven't seen or talked to my parents since they disowned me twenty-two years ago. When did they make this will?"

"The last version was five years ago, but you've been named as the sole heir ever since I started working with them twenty years ago."

"I don't understand."

The attorney nodded towards her purse where she'd stashed the letter, his eyes warm with sympathy.

"I understand that it's all explained in that letter. I know you've had a big shock Ms. Langdon. Why don't you take a few days to process everything, then you can come back and sign all the paperwork to transfer everything over to your name. I'll have my assistant call you tomorrow to schedule something."

She nodded. "OK. Thank you."

Brian stood and helped her to her feet, putting his arm around her and walking her to the elevator. She followed along in a daze. Brian hailed them a cab and she stared out the window in a state of shock until she realized that they had pulled up in front of her townhouse.

Emily walked into her house and flopped down on her couch, resting her head against the back. She could hear Brian puttering around in the kitchen, and he returned a few minutes later with a glass of water and the bottle of whiskey.

"Drink," he said, handing her the water.

They sat there in silence for a few minutes until Brian said, "What do you need Emily? Do you want me to stay? Or I can call Amber and Emily? I feel like you shouldn't be alone."

She looked up at him, her eyes tracing the lines of his handsome face. "I really don't know," she admitted. "Can you stay with me just for a little while? At least until I read the letter?"

"Of course, I'll stay as long as you want me here, honey."

Brian poured them each a shot of whiskey and she sipped hers slowly, relishing the burn in her throat. When she finished it off, she removed the letter from the purse she was still clutching to her side. As she opened the envelope, she realized that her hands were shaking. She took a deep breath, calling on her willpower to stay detached.

Dear Emily,

This letter must come as a shock, given the way we parted.

When you came to us and told us what happened to you, we didn't understand. We were angry, believing that what happened to you was your own fault. It was only a few years later that we began to understand. The daughter of good friends of ours had a similar experience, and the way her parents rallied around her and supported her made us feel ashamed. Years of counseling and reading everything we can about assault have helped us learn where we went wrong, and how much we failed you.

We understand now. We understand that it wasn't your fault. You didn't deserve what happened to you – no one does.

When we kicked you out, we assumed you'd be back, asking for help. We figured we'd work it all out then, but to our shock, you never contacted us again. Every time the phone rang with an unknown number, we hoped it as you. Even though it was what we told you to do, it still hurt that we never heard from you again. We always wondered what had happened to you, and if we would meet our grandchild someday.

A few years ago, we hired a private investigator to tell us where you were and what your life was like. We learned that you are a successful businesswoman, and a homeowner. We also learned that you gave birth to a healthy baby girl who you gave up for adoption. We can only imagine what a heart-wrenching decision that must have been for you, no doubt made worse by our abandonment.

There have been many times over the years that we resolved to reach out, to beg you for forgiveness. We even went to your house once, but we couldn't get the courage up to knock on your door, knowing that we'd made you hate us. If you're reading this letter, then we remained too cowardly to apologize in person – another thing we will apologize to you for.

We know we failed you, but we've both worked very hard over the last twenty years to leave as big of a legacy to our daughter as we could. We can't undo the past Emily, and we know that money won't erase the pain we caused you, but hopefully it will bring you some comfort and additional security.

Hopefully, this inheritance will show that we love you. We always have, and always will.

Mom & Dad

She read the letter once, then again, wondering if her eyes were deceiving her. "What the actual fuck?"

Brian looked at her curiously, and she shoved the letter towards him.

"Are you sure you want me to read this?" he asked softly.

She nodded. He read the letter, then pulled her in for a tight hug. She leaned against him, drawing on his strength. His arms were a safe haven that she never wanted to leave.

She knew she should feel something about the letter from her parents, but mostly she just felt numb. Well, maybe not numb, more like numbly angry. In fact, she was furious.

"I can't believe they thought leaving me money would make up for everything they put me through. That they thought they could buy my forgiveness and I'd be pathetically grateful. Then they have the nerve to tell me that they were hurt that I never came groveling back to them? I should dump their ashes in the damn trash!"

"I'm so sorry, love."

He squeezed her tighter, and suddenly Brian's arms felt too confining, his comfort almost smothering. Maybe she had let this relationship go too far. Brian's declaration of love two nights ago had freaked her out, but not as much as the realization that something had shifted inside her too.

She had tried not to think of it today, but now it hit her like a boot to the head. When she needed comfort last night, she had called him first. She'd called him before Emily and Amber, who'd always been there for her, no matter what. Somehow she'd come to rely on him way more than she ever intended to.

She didn't want to trust her instincts on this. She cared for him, maybe even loved him, but she didn't want to rely on him. She couldn't trust the love and safety he offered. She'd felt safe before, and the very people who were supposed to be there for her had pushed her away at the worst time in her life, and then tried to buy her off and apologize in a letter. A stupid posthumous letter.

Hadn't she learned by now that the only person she could rely on was herself? Had she learned nothing about getting too close to people? Jenny and Amber were closer than family, but they were the exception. They'd proved over and over again that they would support her and be there for her when she needed something. Maybe Brian would be too, but she couldn't take the chance.

"I appreciate you helping me last night and today," she said as she pushed away from him, "but I really need to be alone now."

"Are you sure?" he asked, his gaze concerned.

She nodded. She was struggling to control her breathing and knew she was minutes away from breaking down. She needed to get rid of him.

"Do you want me to call Amber or Jenny to come over?"

She shook her head. "No. Thanks. I just…," she paused and cleared her throat, the fragile control she had on her emotions threatening to break. "I really just need to be alone right now."

He stood up, dropping a kiss on the top of her head. "I understand. If you need anything, just let me know, OK?"

She nodded. Why was he so perfect? A perfect man like Brian needed a perfect woman, not someone whose parents didn't love her and who abandoned their child and who hadn't had a long-term relationship with a man her entire life.

"I'll call you later," he promised. He gave her a lingering look, then to her relief, he left.

The minute the door closed she flopped back against the couch cushions and for the first time in years she allowed herself to cry.

Brian

It had two days since he'd heard from Emily. Forty-eight hours since she told him she wanted to be alone. He'd called and texted her several times, with no response. She was grieving, he knew that, but why wasn't she responding to him? He didn't understand. He'd been the one she called when she heard the news, so why was she avoiding him now?

She was also avoiding Jane. His niece had texted him this afternoon to ask if he'd heard from Emily. Brian wasn't even sure if Jane knew that her grandparents had died, and there was no way he wanted to be the one to break that news. Their history with Emily was way too complicated, and it was up to her how much she wanted to share with her daughter.

He tried Emily's number again and when she didn't answer the phone he decided to head over to her house after work. He knocked on the door, flashing back to the first time he came over with Jane. Emily's house was as comfortable to him as his own now after spending so much time there. Unfortunately they hadn't exchanged keys. Somehow it had never come up. He knocked again and pressed the buzzer at the same time. He was starting to get worried.

Finally the door opened, and his eyes widened. Emily looked terrible. She was still wearing the same wrinkled clothes she'd worn to the attorney's office two days ago. Her hair was sticking out in all directions, and she had dried smudges of make-up under her eyes, dark against her paler than normal skin. She clearly hadn't showered, and he wondered if she'd even eaten.

She stared at him listlessly from the doorway. "Yeah?"

"How are you, love? I was worried when you didn't answer any of my calls or messages."

She sighed sadly. "I don't know where my phone is."

"Have you eaten?" he asked.

She frowned. "I don't remember."

Now he was really worried. The Emily he knew and loved would never miss a meal. She loved to eat. "Can I come in?"

She shook her head and maintained her position blocking the door. "Look Brian, this isn't going to work out."

"I can come back another time."

"No, I mean this relationship. It's...it's not going to work." Her eyes filled with tears, and she choked back a sob, a look of horror on her face.

He reared back in shock. He'd been expecting to come over and comfort her, not get dumped.

"What? Why? I thought things were going well between us."

She shook her head. "Let's not make this more difficult than this is," she sniffed, as if she were trying hard not to cry.

"I know you've had a shock Emily but please, don't throw this relationship away. We're great together."

She shook her head again. "I can't do this."

"I love you."

"I'm sorry, but I just don't feel the same way."

"I don't believe you."

"What?" she gasped. It was the first sign of life he'd seen since she opened the door.

"I refuse to accept your break-up."

"You can't refuse to accept a break-up," she protested.

"Sure I can. We are not breaking up."

"Brian, I'm really sorry. You're a great guy, and I like you a lot, but I can never be what you need. I'm not a relationship person. I'm way too fucked up."

"You already are what I need, and I love you just the way you are." He was feeling increasingly desperate at the determined look in her eyes.

She shook her head sadly. "I'm sorry. I need you to go. Please don't contact me again."

Before he could react, she closed the door in his face. He heard the click of the deadbolt. What the hell had just happened? He stood on the porch staring at the door for several long minutes, trying to figure out his next move.

Finally, he headed for his car, pulling out his phone to call Jane. "Hey, do you have Emily or Amber's numbers?"

Emily

The doorbell rang again about an hour later and Emily swore from her position sprawled on the couch. Why couldn't that guy get a clue? What part of "I'm breaking up with you" hadn't been clear, she wondered.

He started pounding on the door and she pulled the blanket over her head. Maybe if she ignored him he would go away. Then she heard the lock engage and realized that someone with a key was coming in. Brian didn't have a key to her place.

She slid the blanket down underneath her eyes and glared as Jenny and Amber strode into the living room, looking like two women on a mission.

"What are you guys doing here?" she grumbled.

"Never mind that, what the fuck is going on?" Jenny demanded.

"Nothing. Please go away."

Amber pulled the blanket off her and scowled. "Nothing? You're laying here in your own funk wearing clothes that you've obviously been wearing for a few days. Your hair is a rat's nest and no offense, but you stink. Get your ass up and go take a shower."

"Go away," she said weakly.

"No." Amber was in her bossy mood. "Get up now or I swear to god I'll drag your skinny ass into that shower and wash you myself. And brush your damn teeth while you're in there. Your breath is as funky as your B.O."

Emily sighed deeply and sat up with a glare. "First of all, my ass is far from skinny. And second, if you want to see me naked Amber, all you have to do is ask. Why are you here?"

Jenny sat on the coffee table and gave her a sympathetic look. "Brian called us. He told us what happened."

"He had no right to do that."

"He was worried about you," Jenny said softly. "And when you're thinking more clearly I'd love to process the fact that you're so in love with this guy that you called him instead of us when you needed support."

"I'm sorry. And I'm not in love with him."

"Yes you are," Amber snipped. "It's obvious to everyone else except you."

Jenny added, "You don't have to be sorry about not calling us first. I get it. Dave's my first call now too, but that doesn't mean that I love you girls any less. And we do want to hear the whole story from you, but first, for the love of god, Amber is right: you need to take a shower."

Emily trudged into the bathroom and took a long hot shower. She had to admit that getting clean and brushing her teeth made her feel like a whole new woman. When she came back out fifteen minutes later, Amber was in the kitchen cooking eggs and bacon.

"What are you doing?" she asked.

"You need to eat," she said. "Sit down and drink your orange juice."

"I'm not hungry."

"Too bad, you're going to eat."

The room was quiet as she ate, her friends watching her silently. She could feel the concern radiating off of them. She finished the plate of food that Amber gave her, then put it in the dishwasher. Once she returned to the table, Amber gave Emily another stern look. It was funny, because of the three of them, Amber was the most hippy dippy, yet when she felt strongly about something there was no one tougher.

"Spill," she ordered. "Tell us everything."

She told them the whole story, starting with Brian telling me her that he loved her, then coming home to get the letter from the attorney the next day. When she got to the part about the letter from her parents, Emily got up and found it on the floor next to the couch. She handed the rumpled up letter to her friends so they could read it for themselves.

"Assholes," Amber said. "Too chickenshit to apologize but think they can buy forgiveness? Typical."

"What are you going to do now?" Jenny asked her.

"I guess I'll have to go clean out the house. I need to do some paperwork at the attorney's office to get everything transferred over to me, then I can put it on sale. God, the thought of going into that house makes me feel sick."

"Then don't do it," Jenny said.

"What do you mean?"

"You could just ask your realtor to hire someone to clean it out for you."

She considered the suggestion. "I think I'll do that for their vacation home in Florida, but I guess I should see if there's anything I want in there. Jane may want some pictures or something. Or maybe she wants a car. They left me two of them."

"In that case, how about we take the next couple of days off and go through the house together?" Jenny suggested. "With the weekend that'll give us four days, that'll at least give us time to figure out what we need to do there."

"Andy has a friend with a hauling company," Amber added. "I can ask them to bring over a dumpster for us to use."

"You guys would do that?" Emily asked.

Amber smacked her on the arm. "Are you seriously asking us this? After all we've been through together. We're better than sisters, don't you ever forget that."

Emily smiled, feeling lighter for the first time since got the letter from the attorney. "OK then, let's do it."

Brian

Three weeks later...

"Uncle Brian? Are you here? Can I come in?"

"In the living room."

Brian looked up as his niece came into the living room, wrinkling her nose. "Jeez Uncle Brian, it's a nice day. Let's open up the curtains and let some fresh air in here. This place smells funky."

He grimaced as she pulled the curtains open, letting bright sunshine into the living room. Jane looked around, noting the mess of take-out containers and empty beer bottles on the coffee table.

"Good lord, this place is a mess."

She disappeared into the kitchen and raced back in with a trash bag. Sweeping everything into the bag, she headed out the front door again, presumably to drop the bag in the garbage chute. She returned a few minutes later and sat across from Brian, studying him for a long moment before shaking her head.

"I guess I should have come over here sooner instead of believing your texts that everything was fine," she said. "You're a mess."

He rolled his eyes at her. "I'm not a mess. I had a hard week at work."

The truth was his niece was right: he was a mess. He'd gone into work every day but just gone through the motions. It was a miracle that his boss hadn't noticed that he was spending most of his time staring into space. He couldn't sleep, couldn't eat, and had fallen into the worse depression he'd ever experienced. At least when Brian lost his sister he'd had Jane to take care of, which had kept him from completely giving into despair. But now...

"I take it you haven't talked to her?"

Brian shook his head. "I called and texted every day for two weeks begging to talk to her and got no response. For all I know she's blocked my number. I sent flowers, a fruit basket, and several meals because I was afraid she wasn't eating. I got no response at all. Nothing. After a while, a guy gets a clue and understands that he's not wanted."

Jane shook her head, looking exasperated. "What am I going to do with you two?"

"Have you talked to her?" Even through the fog of his depression, he was desperate to know how Emily was doing. He missed her so much, it was a physical ache.

"Yeah, I have," she confirmed. "I have big news, that's part of what I came over to tell you. But also, I felt like you were avoiding me, and I was worried about you. And rightly so, I see now. You're a mess."

"It's not that I was avoiding you," he clarified. "It's just, well I'm having a hard time Jane. I really miss her."

She nodded. "She misses you too, and frankly she's just as much of a mess as you are right now."

"She told you that?" he asked, feeling a glimmer of hope.

"No, but I can tell. Amber and Jenny have been talking about it, and we all think she wants to get back together."

He fell back on the couch, his hope dashed. "Yeah, she has a funny way of showing it. What's your big news?"

"I went online to make my first student loan payment yesterday."

"I'm not sure that qualifies as big news," he said wryly.

"When I pulled up my account, it said my balance was zero."

"What?"

"I know, right? I thought it was a mistake, but it turns out someone paid it in full. Fifty thousand dollars. I guessed immediately it was Emily, and I was right."

"She paid off your loans? That's incredible."

"Not only that, but she also set up a trust fund I can access when I'm thirty. It's worth one million dollars," she squealed. "Can you freaking believe that?"

Before he could respond, Jane continued, "I think you heard that her parents left her a bunch of money, so she decided to use some of it to help me since she wasn't around when I was a kid."

"That's awesome honey, I'm so glad. With your parents being upside down on their mortgage when they died and you needing to use that life insurance money for tuition, it'll be nice to have some economic security in case of an emergency."

"I had breakfast with her today."

"You did?" He closed his eyes as a sharp pain ripped through his chest. He and Emily always loved going out for breakfast; it was her favorite meal.

"Yeah. She told me about the trust and gave me a bunch of family pictures she got from her parents' house. She also told me I can have one of their cars since I don't have one. I'm going out there tomorrow to pick one out and see if there's anything else I want from the house before she finishes the paperwork to transfer the property."

"Wow, that's great pumpkin."

"She and Jenny and Amber have been working like mad to clean that house out for the last few weeks. I guess my grandparents were low level hoarders. They filled up a couple of dumpsters and even Dave an Andy were helping. I told Emily that she should have called us, that we would have helped too."

He nodded. "She put the house up for sale?"

Jane shook her head. "No, she donated it to Illinois Women's Services. It's a statewide organization that helps survivors of rape and sexual assault. It's a pretty big house. Emily said they're going to use it as kind of a halfway house for people who need a place to stay while they're recovering from assault."

"Wow, that's really nice."

He loved that Emily was using the property that she'd inherited from her parents to help other girls who were in the same situation as she'd been in so many years ago.

"Aren't you going to ask me?"

"Ask you what?"

"If Emily asked about you."

"No." Brian paused. "Why, did she?"

Jane nodded. "She's miserable without you. You're miserable without her. I'm probably violating the girl code here, but I really care about both of you, and I think you're perfect for each other, so I'm just going to tell you that Emily seems like she really regrets breaking up with you. I thought she was going to cry when your name came up in conversation. Amber thinks she wants to get back together but she's too nervous to approach you after how she treated you."

He shook his head. "Thanks, but Emily has made it really clear the last three weeks that she's done with me."

His niece studied him for a long while. "OK, well I think you're wrong but I'm not going to interfere. If you two prefer to be alone and miserable, who am I to argue?"

Emily

"Reservations for Jane Scott."

"Of course ma'am, this way please."

Emily looked around as she followed the maître d to their table. She hadn't been to this restaurant before. It was located on the main floor of one of the fancy boutique hotels that had sprung up downtown over the last twenty years. The interior was intimate with dim lights and high backed leather booths that offered privacy. It was the kind of restaurant you went to for a romantic date not a "thank you" dinner with your daughter.

Jane had been adamant that she wanted to take Emily out to dinner to thank her for paying off Jane's student loans and giving her a car. She'd tried to gracefully refuse, but her daughter was as stubborn as she was.

Emily started to slide into a booth in the corner when she realized it wasn't Jane who was sitting across from her. It was Brian. She paused with one butt cheek on the seat and one hanging over the edge.

"Brian? What are you doing here?"

He looked as surprised as she did. "Jane asked me to meet her here for dinner," he said. "She was fairly insistent that she wanted to buy me an early birthday dinner."

"When's your birthday?" she asked.

"Next month."

Emily frowned. "Is Jane joining us then?"

Brian shrugged. "No clue." He nodded at the approaching waitress. "Should we order a drink while we figure it out?"

"Good evening, can I get you started with drinks?"

Brian narrowed his eyes and studied the waitress. "Gabby? Is that you?"

The young woman smiled. "Hi Mr. McKenna. I didn't think you'd remember me." She turned to Emily. "You must be Jane's mom. Nice to meet you Ms. Langdon. I'm Gabby."

"What's going on?" She looked between Brian and Gabby in confusion. Brian just shrugged, looking like he was in the dark too.

"Let me get your drinks and then I'll share the next part," Gabby said.

"There's a next part?" Emily asked.

When Gabby just stared at her, she sighed and said, "I'll have a Glenlivet on the rocks please."

"Same here," Brian added.

Gabby hustled off. "I'm confused."

Brian met her gaze, his expression unreadable. "Me too."

Gabby returned with two glasses and an envelope. "Your explanation. I'll be back in a few minutes with your food."

Emily grabbed the envelope from the waitress and opened the note, reading it silently.

"What does it say?" Brian asked.

She read it aloud:

"*Uncle Brian and Emily, you two need help. You're both a mess, and it's time I intervene. It's obvious to all of us that you're in love with each other. You belong together but you two are the only ones who can't figure that out. You've both been totally pathetic since you broke up and we are all tired of it. You want to get back together, you need to get back together, and yet you each stubbornly refuse to make a move. So now I'm making a move for you. Dinner is paid for. So is room 1720 upstairs. Talk. Have dinner. Talk some more. Then go upstairs and make up. Please, we're all begging you to work this out. Love, Jane (and Jenny and Amber too).*"

Emily tipped the envelope over and a hotel key card fell out. "Um, so this is weird."

"Yeah."

Emily took a drink of her scotch, relishing the feeling of the warmth sliding down her throat.

"How have you been?" she asked quietly.

She examined him in the dim light, noting that he had shadows under his eyes, and he looked like he'd lost weight. She knew that look – she saw it in the mirror every day.

"Terrible. You?"

"Same."

He took a long sip of his drink. "I miss you."

She felt something loosen in her chest. The truth was, she'd missed him terribly. Even through the haze of her grief over the revelations from her parents, she'd missed him. Breaking up with him had been an impulsive decision driven by fear, and pride had kept her from reaching out to see if they could have a second chance. Now her daughter was giving her that second chance. She couldn't blow it.

"I miss you too," she said softly.

He leaned forward, placing his elbows on the table, his expression a mixture of surprise and hope.

"I'm sorry Brian. I know I hurt you when I broke up with you. The truth is, I hurt myself as well. All you did was try to take care of me and I acted like an asshole."

"Why did you break up with me?"

She stared at him for a long moment, gathering her courage. "You told me you loved me."

"Yeah, that was a dick move," he said wryly.

She smiled. "It scared me, and then when I got the letter from the lawyer you were the first person I called. I called you instead of Amber and Jenny, and then I started thinking that I was getting too dependent on you. I've been on my own for a long time, it freaked me out."

They paused as Gabby brought the two plates of food they hadn't ordered. At their curious look she shared, "Jane pre-ordered for you."

When the waitress left again, Brian said, "You haven't really been on your own though, have you? You've always had Jenny and Amber. What's wrong with adding to that group?"

"Nothing I guess. I was so turned around about what happened with my parents. It brought up so many confusing emotions. I convinced myself that you would hurt me if I trusted you too much, that one day you would realize that I was just too fucked up for someone like you and reject me. I wasn't thinking straight."

"And now?"

"And now what?"

"Are you thinking straight now?" he asked.

She nodded. "I think so."

She took a bite of her risotto, realizing it was the first thing that had tasted good in weeks.

"I decided to donate my parents' house to help sexual assault survivors," she told him.

"I heard. I also heard about Jane's student loans, and the trust fund. That was incredibly generous of you."

"It was the least I could do for my daughter."

"Actually, the least you could do was nothing at all. Giving her a million dollars is far from the least you could do."

He shot her a grin, and she was struck by how handsome he was. He was kind of a sneaker handsome. Sometimes he just looked like another guy, then he'd smile, and that little dimple would appear in his cheek and his eyes would flash and she'd feel breathless.

She'd missed him. Being away from him was like losing a limb. The memory of having him was almost worse than the pain of not having him.

"What would a girl need to do to get a second chance with a guy like you?" she asked, deciding to be brave. He'd always been the one to take the risks in their relationship. Now it was her turn.

"Well, it depends on the girl." His gaze was teasing.

"What does this girl need to do?"

"Promise to never shut me out again. Promise me that you're in this relationship for the long haul."

She slid out of the booth and moved over to his. "I'm in this for the long haul, because I love you Brian McKenna," she whispered.

His eyes widened and darkened. He laced his fingers through hers. "I love you too Emily. I love you so much."

He leaned forward and kissed her long and hard. When they broke apart, Gabby was at their table with boxes.

"You guys might want to take your food to go. You'll need your energy, I'm guessing."

She laughed and spun away, before turning back. "Jane paid for everything, including my tip. Enjoy your night."

"Did my daughter just 'parent trap' us?" Emily asked as she grabbed her plate and boxed up her food.

"Yep."

"What are we going to do about her?" she asked.

"Ask her to stand up in our wedding?"

She whipped her head around. "Well, you move fast, don't you?"

"Can't take a chance on you changing your mind again," he told her.

"How about we take it one step at a time?" Emily slid out of the booth and pulled his hand. "In the meantime, let's go make use of that free hotel room."

Epilogue – Brian

One year and one month later...

"When are you going to make an honest woman out of my mother?"

Brian looked up as Jane sat down across from him at the kitchen table. The sun was shining through the kitchen window, and it lit up his niece's hair making her look like an angel.

They had all gone to Emily's condo in Florida together to celebrate his birthday. Originally Emily had planned to sell her parents' place but after seeing it, she'd changed her mind. It was a beautiful two-bedroom condo in a sweet location right on the beach, too nice to part with. This was the fourth time they'd visited in the past year. When they weren't there, she was able to rent it out to vacationing guests for extra money which paid for the upkeep and the condo fees.

"Still trying to stage manage our relationship?" Brian teased her.

"I'm just saying, you've been dating for almost a year and a half, what's the delay? You're not getting any younger you know."

Brian sighed, then got up and grabbed a box of Muesli.

"I can't believe you eat that stuff, it's so gross."

Brian smiled and lifted the bag out of the cereal box, pulling out a black velvet box he'd hidden underneath. He slid it across the table towards his niece.

"Oooh, finally!" she said delightedly.

She opened the box and looked at the tasteful diamond engagement ring. "This is beautiful. I love it."

"Are you two getting married now?"

They both jumped when the heard Emily's voice. She looked adorably rumpled in a pair of sleep shorts and one of his t-shirts, her feet bare.

"Oh. Crap. I didn't know you were up."

She'd been up late last night working so he figured that she would sleep in today. It wasn't even seven o'clock.

Emily shuffled to the coffee pot and poured herself a cup before returning to the table. He and Jane sat there, frozen, the ring on the table between them.

Emily picked up the ring box and looked at it approvingly. "Nice choice."

Brian cleared his throat, suddenly more nervous than he'd ever been in his life. He wasn't sure why; they were already living together, getting married wasn't a reach.

"The ring is for you."

"I hope so," Emily said teasingly. "I know we're in the south but even here they would frown on a guy marrying his niece."

Jane got up with a wide smile. "I'm going to take a walk on the beach. I'll be gone at least an hour if you have anything you need to celebrate."

She grabbed her bag and scurried out of the condo. Emily looked at him expectantly, but when he just sat there nervously she put him out of his misery.

"Hey Brian, would you marry me?"

He smiled, relief coursing through his body. "Yes. Will you marry me?"

"Yes."

He pulled her up to give her a kiss, then slid the ring on her finger.

"I only have one question," she asked. "Is Jane going to stand up for you or for me at the wedding?"

"We can flip for it," he whispered, giving her another kiss. He couldn't believe she'd said yes. Even after all this time together, he'd still be afraid she'd freak out.

"Just promise me one thing," she said.

"Anything."

"When Jane falls in love, you and I are totally going to meddle."

***

Did you like this book? Show the love and leave me a review. Reviews are like puppies, they make you feel happy.

Keep reading for a special excerpt from "Until You Came Along", available now from select retailers. And be sure to Join my mailing list[1] to keep up on all my new releases.

---

1.   *https://storyoriginapp.com/giveaways/62ee758e-068f-11eb-904e-c373f6014fe1*

Special Preview

Until You Came Along by Rose Bak

Jen heard the rumbling from all the way in the kitchen. Wiping her hands on a towel, she walked to the front porch to watch the two large buses drive up the long driveway to the farmhouse. Belching smoke, they idled and came to a stop, one behind the other.

Although it wasn't even 10 a.m. yet, the sun shone brightly in the summer sky, showcasing the dust left in the wake of the parked buses. A bird squawked loudly in the sudden silence as a serious looking young woman scurried out of the first bus, glasses askew, a clipboard gripped in one hand, cellphone in another. Two large mountains of men followed her, hulking shadows.

"Jen Oliver? The band is here. We'll just come in and...." she moved to enter the house, but Jen stood her ground, blocking the door.

"Where are they?" she asked the woman, her tone icy. "And who are you exactly?"

The woman looked flustered for a brief moment before her stern mask fell back down again. She shuffled her cell phone into the hand with the clipboard and stuck out her now-free hand to shake. "I'm Simone. I manage the band."

Jen ignored her hand. "Well, manage them out of those buses. They don't get to send the help out to greet their sister."

Simone looked confused as she dropped her hand back to her side. "They're all sleeping. They had a late night. We'll just come in and check...."

"Still up all night and sleeping all day, huh? That's been the same since they were teenagers." Jen shook her head. On the farm they had all been taught the value of hard work – up before dawn, work all day, and early to bed. Somehow those lessons hadn't really stuck with her brothers despite her grandparents' best efforts over the years.

Of course, the boys, as she still thought of them, had been away from the farm for ten years now, chasing fame and fortune as the biggest boy band to hit the charts since N Sync. Like the band that came before them, the Oliver Boys had grown up but continued to enchant teenage girls across the world with their pop tunes.

Simone clearly felt protective of the boys. "They played last night in Wichita you know," she said sternly. "The show went until almost midnight, then they met the fans and press for hours after."

"By meet the fans and press do you mean got drunk and partied?" Jen's tone did little to hide her opinion of the boys and their reputation for debauched partying.

Simone shook her head. "They've mostly settled down now. There's not as much partying as there used to be when they were younger. But they still need to make an effort to meet people, it's part of the job. Now we'll just come in and...."

Jen shook her head. "Well," she drawled. "When they wake up from their so-called job, you send them on in. The rest of you need to find some other place to bunk. I'm not running a hotel for drunken roadies here."

A slight movement behind Simone caught Jen's eyes. One of the giant men flanking Simone shook with repressed laughter, his mouth twisted in a smirk but his face otherwise impassive. Jen looked at him for the first time. He was the size of a small tank, several inches over six feet tall, with impossibly wide shoulders and large biceps. His hair was a dark blond, "dishwater blonde" her grandma would call it, worn military short. He was dressed all in black, and she noticed a gun on the shoulder holster. Jen wondered why he felt he needed a gun out here in the middle of nowhere. She felt him watching her and she raised her eyes to his, a shiver of awareness coursing through her, although she couldn't make out his eyes behind the dark sunglasses.

"Miss Oliver..." Simone started again.

"Jen"

"OK, then, Jen, we need to do a security sweep before the boys come in. If you could just move aside, we'll get started." Simone nodded decisively.

"A security—-what the hell are you talking about?"

Simone turned to the man who'd been staring at Jen earlier. "This is Nick, he's head of security for the band. He'll be doing a security sweep and assessment with Brian here," she pointed at the second silent man.

"We don't need a security sweep. This place is as safe as it comes. We don't even lock the doors in these parts."

Simone shook her head again, vibrating with irritation and clearly not used to people disobeying her orders. "No way. The boys don't go anywhere without a security check ahead of time. I'm afraid I have to insist."

Jen shot her a look filled with venom, her tone as cold as ice. "You can insist all you like but this is my property. You have no right to it, and neither do the boys. Y'all can just run along now, I'm not having some ginormous strangers poking around my property. Don't make me sic the dogs on you." Simone's mouth dropped open.

This was an empty threat. Jen's three dogs looked mean, but they were incurably friendly. They were just as likely to lick a person to death as bite them. Jen had a sneaking suspicion that if someone tried to kill her the dogs would jump over her body and leave with the killer. But these music people didn't need to know that. If there was one thing Jen hated, it was music people. They were way too self-important and proud.

"Excuse me ma'am," the guy called Nick interrupted.

"Jen," she repeated, a trace of irritation in her tone.

He inclined his head. "Sorry. Jen. As Simone mentioned, I'm head of security for the band. We've had some issues and I would be very appreciative if my team could just poke around for a bit and make sure there's nothing amiss." His tone was deferential and charming, which only heightened Jen's suspicions.

"What kind of issues?"

"I'm afraid I'm not at liberty to discuss that ma—I mean Jen."

"Then I'm afraid I'm not at liberty to grant you access to my property. You step foot off that driveway, and I'll shoot you myself, right after I set the dogs on you. And you," she pointed at Simone, "better make sure no one bothers me again until I see those boys on my porch." She spun on her heel and slammed the door. It was going to be a long day.

***

For more of Jen's story, check out Until You Came Along by Rose Bak. Available at select online retailers.

Other Books by Rose Bak

The Diamond Bay Contemporary Romance Series
Brand New Penny
Fresh as a Daisy
Right as Rain
Bite-Sized Shifters Paranormal Romance Series
Wolf Doctor
Kat's Dog
Designer Wolf
Wolf Sheriff
The Good with Numbers Holiday Romance Series
Love Unmasked
The Thanksgiving Scrooge
Maid for Christmas
Countdown to Love
Valentine's Lottery
The Oliver Boys Band Contemporary Romance Series
Until You Came Along
Rock Star Teacher
Rock Star Writer
Rock Star Neighbor
Loving the Holidays Contemporary Romance Series
Dating Santa
New Year's Steve
Independence Dave
Beach Wedding
Together Again
Non-fiction
What to Do If You Find a Cougar in Your Living Room: Self-Care in an Uncaring World

Catch up with these and other stories coming soon. Join my newsletter for more information[1] or follow my author page on your favorite retailer.

---

1. *https://storyoriginapp.com/giveaways/62ee758e-068f-11eb-904e-c373f6014fe1*

About the Author

Rose Bak has been obsessed with books since she got her first library card at age five. She is a passionate reader with an e-reader bursting with thousands of beloved books.

Although Rose enjoys writing both fiction and nonfiction, romance novels have always been her favorite guilty pleasure, both as a reader and an author. Rose's contemporary romance books focus on strong female characters over thirty-five and the alpha males who love them. Expect a lot of steam, a little bit of snark, and a guaranteed happily ever after.

Rose lives in the Pacific Northwest with her family, and special needs dogs. In addition to writing, she also teaches accessible yoga and loves music. Sadly, she has absolutely no musical talent, so she mostly sings in the shower.

Please sign up for my newsletter[1] to get a free book and keep up to date on all the Rose Bak romance news.

---

1. *https://storyoriginapp.com/giveaways/62ee758e-068f-11eb-904e-c373f6014fe1*